the Wise Enchanter

the Wise Enchanter

A JOURNEY THROUGH THE ALPHABET

written by Shelley Davidow
illustrated by Krystyna Emilia Kurzyca

BELL POND BOOKS

FOR

Autumn, Isaac, Emory, Merik, Sarina, Timothy, Sadie, Mikail, Morgan and Lilliana.

AND IN LOVING MEMORY OF

Birgit Bernatzeder

Published by Bell Pond Books
610 Main Street, Great Barrington MA 01230

www.bellpondbooks.com

Library of Congress Cataloging-in-Publication Data

Davidow, Shelley, 1969-
The wise enchanter : a journey through the alphabet / written by Shelley Davidow ; illustrated by Krystyna Emilia Kurzyca.
p. cm.
Summary : As his days grow short and the Cloud of Ignorance suddenly becomes more dense, the Wise Enchanter sends his daughter, Gadrun, to find four children who can defeat Urckl, the Master of Ignorance and Shadows, by rediscovering the alphabet and stories.
ISBN 0-88010-562-3
[1. Wisdom—Fiction. 2. Adventure and adventurers—Fiction. 3. Alphabet—Fiction. 4. Storytelling—Fiction. 5. Books and reading —Fiction. 6. Fairy tales.] I. Kurzyca, Krystyna Emilia, ill. II. Title.
PZ7.D28235Wis 2005
[Fic]—dc22

2005027506

10 9 8 7 6 5 4 3 2 1

Printed in the United States of America

Acknowledgements

Thanks to Stan Maher who was there at the very beginning; to Beth Robbins whose enthusiasm and insights made this book possible; to Ruth Gundle and the V.I.P. Group (Very Important Poultry Group), Bette Husted, Ursula K. Le Guin, Judith Barrington, Molly Gloss, and Caroline Le Guin for their invaluable support, wit and Wisdom, which has so illuminated my writing journey over the last few years; to Carol and David Liknaitzky, and Bob and Maureen Davidow for showing me courage; and to Paul and Tim Williams for their love.

I'd also like to extend my gratitude to everyone at Bell Pond Books: Mary Giddens, Stephan O' Reilly, Christopher Bamford, Gene Gollogly, William (Jens) Jensen, and Andy Flaxman. Thank you!

prologue

ONCE UPON A TIME, on a magical island that could be reached only sometimes and by very few people, lived a Wise Enchanter, old and as wise as the sky. His castle rose high above the silvery beach and waves—so high that its tall spires often disappeared in the mists that frequently hid the island from view. Now, this Wise Enchanter was the last of the Wise Enchanters. He knew the time would come when he would be old and go to the Everlasting Islands, and new wise men and women would be needed to oversee the lands and make sure that Wisdom did not die.

One day the Wise Enchanter looked out over the wide oceans. His heart felt heavy. In the distance, just above the horizon, hung a single, dark cloud.

"Gadrun," he called. "Come, listen to me."

Gadrun was the Enchanter's beautiful daughter. She was so beautiful that even the rosy dawn, spreading across the world each morning, drew in its breath when it saw her.

Gadrun ran to her father. A frown creased her brow. "Dear father," she said. "I see that you are worried."

"I am getting old," he replied. "Without Wisdom, there can be no new Enchanters after I am gone. No children have come to my island for many years. It is happening just as I feared. Wisdom is fading in the world. Words are disappearing. The brightness in the sky is vanishing and the dark Cloud of Ignorance has grown suddenly dense. A new darkness is looming. Someone is being created in the deep. He is growing stronger every minute. If he is not stopped, he will grow immense. If he grows strong enough, he will rise up and devour every word and sound. The earth will become a cold, silent place, too terrible to imagine."

"Who are you talking about?" Gadrun whispered.

"I do not like to utter his name," her father whispered. "But I will say it for you. His name is the Master of Ignorance and Shadows. His name is Urckl!"

Gadrun grew pale and silent at the mention of Urckl. Once, some time ago, Urckl had found enough strength to send one of his messengers to the end of the world. Something terrible had happened then in the Enchanted Islands and Gadrun's heart had been broken.

"Father," she said, looking deep into his eyes, "You are wise beyond measure." You must know what to do. Tell me how I can help. Tell me what to do and I will do it. We will stop this shadow."

Her father looked at her sadly but kindly. "Thank you Gadrun; we will try our best. We must find those who are young enough to rediscover the world. Every letter, every sound must be found anew and made bright again. You and I cannot do it. Only the very young can face such a challenge. Children, who are still full of wonder, could do it! I want you to go off into the world. Use whatever shape you must, but find me four children from the four corners of the earth who are kind and true, who have wonder in their hearts and are neither selfish nor unkind—and who will be brave enough to go on a quest."

"What will they be looking for? Where must they go?" asked Gadrun.

"Their task will be to rediscover the alphabet and bring back what is being lost. They must listen to stories, listen to the old people, ask questions, and heed the answers. Only then will the darkness be overcome. Only then will children find their way once more to my castle.

Then, and only then, will wise men and women return to the world. We will have to use many kinds of magic, and yet we are quite powerless to stop this darkness ourselves. So, my dear Gadrun, when you have found the right children, bring them together. Listen to the questions in their hearts, for they must be full of questions. Then help them begin their journey. Every letter they learn and love will bring them a step closer to the Enchanted Islands. Every time they learn something new, the world will grow lighter and the sun brighter. But if they should fail, the clouds that are beginning to form as the result of people's murky thoughts will increase. Light and warmth will vanish. The world will fall into an icy grip of eternal cold, and Urckl will grow strong enough to come up from the deep to devour the whole, bright, beautiful world. Go now, Gadrun. Be careful, but be as quick as you can."

Gadrun said goodbye to her father. She ran down the steps of the castle onto the beach and leapt into the waves. Instantly, she became a dolphin, and began to swim away from the island with all her might.

As she traveled the oceans of the world (she could travel much faster than any ordinary dolphin) she learned something from the fish and the whales and the whispers of the men and women on the big ships and boats that passed overhead. She visited many beaches and searched with keen eyes and ears for children who had wonder in their hearts and who were neither selfish nor unkind. But for a long while, she could not find them.

Everywhere she went, even children who seemed at first to be full of wonder, showed themselves to be unkind, or selfish. Gadrun began to despair of even finding one child, never mind four.

One day she learned of a city next to a warm sea where four children, one from each corner of the earth, already knew each other, were friends, and played together. Gadrun even heard their names whispered across the moonlit waves.

"These four children are the best of friends. Michael is six and a half. He was born in the western part of the world, in America. Lauren is seven. She was born in the far north, in Scotland, but now she lives next door to Michael. Rukmini is seven, too. She comes from the east, from India. Her parents came west in a big ship when she was five. Sipho is almost seven. He lived in the south, in Africa, until he was six. Now he plays ball with Michael every day."

When Gadrun heard these whispers, she swam right to the bay where the children played in the evenings. There, while she was swimming around among the coral reefs waiting for the children, she met a sea sprite. Gadrun told the sprite her story.

"I will help you if I can, for I, too, have heard the rumblings of Urckl," said the sea sprite, and she followed the dolphin toward the shore.

The sun dipped its golden rays into the water when the children ran down onto the sand. Gadrun listened to them talk and watched them play. They were kind and unselfish. She heard not a single unkind word pass between them. They certainly had wonder in their hearts.

Most importantly, however, Gadrun heard their many questions—for that morning, as on most mornings, the children were full of questions.

"Why is the sky blue?" Michael asked.

"What is the biggest number in the whole world?" Rukmini asked.

"Why do my eyes blink?" asked Lauren.

"Is there someone who knows everything in the world?" Sipho asked.

"Maybe dolphins do," said Rukmini. "Look, a dolphin is swimming close to the shore. Let's go see it!"

They ran splashing into the waves. They were most surprised when the dolphin began to swim toward them. The next minute, one by one, they were lifted onto the dolphin's back. The children shrieked with delight and held on tight.

"A tame dolphin," Lauren said and patted the sleek head. "Dolphin," she continued. "Can you help us answer our questions?"

The dolphin seemed to nod. "Look, she understands us. She's taking us somewhere."

With the children on her back, the dolphin swam out to the coral reef. Reaching it, the children saw a beautiful being sitting on a rock in the middle of the ocean.

"Look, a mermaid!" they shouted.

"No," said the being in a shimmering, silvery voice. "I am a sea sprite."

"Do you know the answers to all questions?" asked Sipho.

"No," said the sprite. "But I can send you on your way to find them. You must find the castle of the Wise Enchanter. He alone can help you."

"What must we do? How do we get there?" asked Rukmini. She stroked the dolphin's back.

"It is a long journey. On the way, listen to the words of old people. Look at the world around you, and learn from it. When you know as much as you can know, and when you have found what must be found, you will begin to understand how your questions might be answered. Then you will be ready to find the castle of the Wise Enchanter."

The children's eyes opened wide. The sea sprite smiled kindly and disappeared into the waves. The dolphin leapt and turned around in the waves and hastened back to the shore. She lowered herself down and let the children slide off her back. Each child stroked her shiny skin, and then Gadrun waved good-bye with her tail.

"Come," said Lauren, bounding out of the sea. "We have to listen to the stories of old people, and begin our journey as soon as we may."

As soon as Gadrun heard this, she spun around in the water and sent a shower of sunlit droplets into the air. Then she swam back to her father's island as fast as she could to tell him what she had found.

"Well done, my child," the Wise Enchanter said. "And now we will wait and watch the sea and the sky."

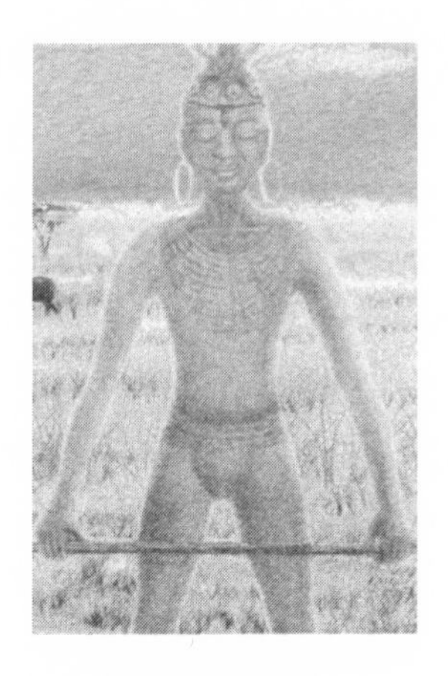

one

As Sipho put his head down on his pillow, he immediately began to drift back to Africa, to the place where he had been born. It was the first day of the long school holidays. Sipho was tired after his adventure with the dolphin and the sea sprite and had more questions than ever that needed to be answered, so he went to bed early.

Often he dreamed of the giant trees and rolling hills of Zululand, and on this particular night, he dreamt of the rocks and waving grasses behind his family's old mud hut. He dreamed that he walked out into the warm, starry evening, carrying his sleeping mat, to lie down under the stars. As he lay down on the mat, he heard a deep voice. "Sipho," it said, and seemed to rumble like the distant thunder of the first summer rain. When he looked up at the night sky, he saw a handsome warrior standing in shimmering starlight.

"Who are you?" Sipho asked.

"I am your ancestor. I am your father's father's father's father's father's father. Do not forget where you have come from."

"I won't forget. Why are you here?" he asked, and shivered, though it wasn't at all cold.

"Because I've heard the many questions in your heart."

"Can you tell me the answers?"

"No. I am here to give you courage. Only you can make the journey of learning that leads to Wisdom and only with Wisdom you will find the answers that you seek. You and your friends must make this journey. When you wake up, you will remember that your task will be to make pictures of all that you find on your way, until you have filled a book. You must look carefully to find the secret signs that will unlock the Wisdom of the world. There are twenty-six symbols in all, and you must uncover every one. Then, when the book is heavy and full, you might find what you have been searching for. Remember, I am here, Sipho. You may always find me. I am your ancestor, ancient, and ageless. Wherever you are, I am."

Sipho heard the deep voice grow fainter, and when he turned his head, his ancestor was gone. The mat felt very soft underneath him. Slowly, he opened his eyes and saw that he was far away from Africa, lying not on a grass mat, but in a bed with blue and white sheets in a house where the morning sun was shining brightly through the window, and the warm voices of his parents were drifting toward him from the kitchen.

Later that morning the four friends met down on the beach. Sipho told his friends his dream. They listened carefully. "And so," Sipho said, "I know what we have to do. We have to make a magic book. We must fill it with the things we find along the way. We must look for the twenty six symbols that will unlock the Wisdom of the world."

"Yes!" exclaimed Lauren. "And I have just the book. After the beach, come back to my house. I'll show you."

So, when it was time for lunch, the children went to Lauren's house. In her bedroom, she took a large, heavy book from her shelf. It was a beautiful, handmade book, with a leather cover embossed with intricate golden designs. Lauren opened it carefully. The book was full of blank pages just waiting to be filled.

"My mother made this," Lauren said. "She said it was to be used for something special. I haven't found anything special enough for such a book, yet."

"But now we do have something special enough," Sipho said as Lauren flipped through the many clean pages. "Yes, this is the book, the Magic Book."

The others all looked at the book. It seemed suddenly alive with magical possibilities. The golden designs on the cover shimmered.

Lauren flipped to the first smooth, clean white page. Then she carefully took out her best crayons from a drawer next to her bed and handed them to Sipho.

"You start, Sipho. Put something on the first page."

And Sipho began. He drew his ancestor in Africa coming to him in a dream. When he was finished, he looked at his friends. The drawing was so beautiful that no one could believe what they were seeing. Sipho himself could hardly believe what he had drawn.

"I drew this, and yet I couldn't have! Look what he gave us," Sipho said, and showed them his ancestor standing there so straight, with his assegai held firmly in both hands. "He is standing like an A. He's my ancestor. He's always there when I need him."

The children stared in astonishment. They all took turns tracing with their fingers the beautiful letter A that they saw in the ancestor.

"I've never been able to draw like this before," Sipho said softly. "There is something extraordinary about this book."

"It's magic," Lauren said. "It's not just any old book."

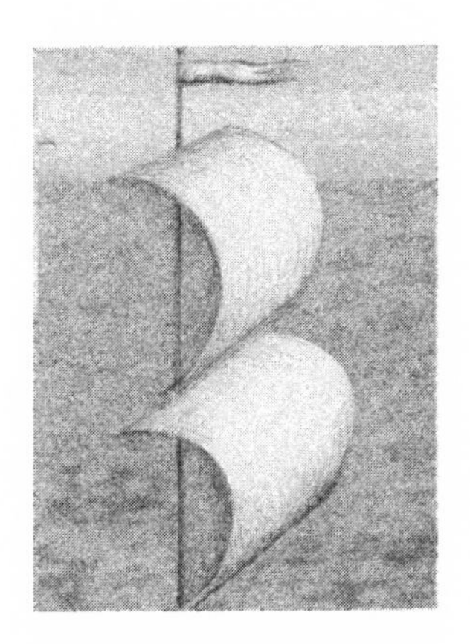

two

"BOAT-BUILDING isn't easy," Sipho announced. "And I think we'll need a boat for what we have to do." He sighed. "You see, I'm sure it's going to be a long journey to find the castle of the Wise Enchanter. And if he lives on an island, we can only go by sea."

"You're right," said Rukmini. "But we won't have to build a whole boat! My grandpa has a sailing boat, which just needs a little work. We can sand off the old paint and refinish it. There's a hole where a knot of wood fell out. We could seal that. We could mend the sail with sheets. Then we would have a beautiful, big sailing boat. We could sail to the end of the world and find the Wise Enchanter. My Grandpa's a sailor. I can ask him to teach us about boat-building and sailing."

"We'll need our boat to be big and strong to hold all of us and all our things," Michael said. "Is it a big boat? It'll need a tall sail to catch the wind and take us far across the sea."

"It's big, but not too big. We could sail it if we learn how."

And so, that very day, the four friends went to ask Rukmini's Grandfather about the boat. He was excited by what he heard and said he would be happy to take them to where it lay beached near some sand dunes waiting to be fixed up.

"I've been waiting for someone to come and give this old friend a helping hand. If you can fix it, I'll teach you to sail it," he said, and his eyes shone with good humor.

Rukmini's Grandpa gave them sand paper and taught them how to work with the wood. He gave them a jar of sticky roofing tar and taught them how to seal the cracks and stop the gaps. He gave them special blue and white paint and some brushes. They worked hard, stopping only to drink or to eat a sandwich.

"What about this hole where the knot of wood fell out?" Lauren asked.

"The lid of the tar jar is exactly the right size," Michael said, and pushed it into the hole where it fit snugly.

"Now we can seal that with tar," Sipho said and did an excellent job fixing it.

They tarred the gaps and sanded the old mast until it was smooth. They worked for days, from early in the morning as the sun came over the green treetops to just after the sun dipped orange into the silvery sea. People watched the busy children. Sometimes they stopped, but the children were so hard at work they barely noticed.

Even though it was hot and the children were tired, they were kind to each other all the time. No one shouted and no one got upset when things didn't work just as they wanted them to.

At last it was time to paint the boat and fix the sails, and when that was done and the boat was blue with fine white trim, they climbed into it. Laughing, they hoisted the sails on the boat, which still sat proudly on the dune. That evening as the sun went down, the children were tired but satisfied with the work they had done.

"It really looks like a boat now!" said Lauren.

"We still have to learn how to sail it," Sipho said.

"Tonight I'll ask my grandfather about sailing, and tomorrow he can show us," said Rukmini.

The next morning the air was cool and fresh. The four friends waited excitedly by the boat for Rukmini's grandfather to arrive. It was the perfect day for learning how to sail.

"Such hard workers," her Grandpa said, eyeing the careful paint job and the perfectly mended sails. "Such good workers! Let's see if she sails. Rukmini my dear, are you ready?"

"I'm ready, Grandpa!"

"I'm going to take her out a little way, then bring her back if everything's okay. And then you can come with me."

"Okay, Grandpa!"

The wind blew and blew and buffeted the boat in the bay.

"It's a good boat," Rukmini's grandfather called out over the wind. Then he sailed back to the shore. Rukmini waded through the water to meet him.

"I'll take you, Rukmini. I'll show you all I can. Then you will be able to show your friends."

Rukmini climbed into the boat with her Grandpa's help. Michael and Lauren and Sipho waved, and Rukmini watched them until they were dots and the shore disappeared in the distance.

The big blue expanse of water spread out as far as the eye could see. Seagulls dipped and fished, and giant pelicans bobbed along the waves like royal gentlemen, inspecting what swam below the surface of the water with their keen, sharp eyes.

"It may be a good boat," Rukmini called back, "but it rocks too much!" The old man smiled.

"Be brave, my young sailor. Even the best boat rocks. As long as it floats and sails, it's doing the right thing."

A big gust filled the sails and they billowed out, full of air. "Oh, look how big and how beautiful the sails are, Grandpa!"

"Yes, they're strong. Look how they catch the wind and how we can race across the waves."

"You're a good sailor, Grandpa!"

"And you are too, Rukmini."

"Not as good as you."

"Not yet. But you will be. Look! Now we're sailing with the wind. Next, I'll show you how to tack against the wind. You might need to do that someday."

All day Rukmini learned from her grandfather. The wind became a friend who tickled and played and pushed and pulled the boat along, and who whooshed and whined and even rattled sometimes. All the while, the sea churned white behind them. Blue and green swells held the boat from both sides. Suddenly, a dark shadow swept over the water. Rukmini looked up to see if a cloud had crossed the sun, but the sky was clear and blue.

"Grandpa, are there any sea monsters in the sea?"

"I haven't seen one yet, my dear."

"I thought I saw a huge green tail sweep across the water."

"It was probably a giant piece of sea weed."

"Probably."

"Or our own shadow."

"Yes, it could have been."

On the way back to the shore at the end of the day, Rukmini looked at the billowing sails and said: "Grandpa, look, the boat's big billowing sails are showing us something."

"What is it?"

"Oh, it's so exciting. It's as exciting as learning to sail! I must tell Sipho and Michael and Lauren. We will have to put it into our book."

They could both see the beach now, but there was no sign of Sipho, Lauren, and Michael. They had all gone home once they'd seen Rukmini out into the bay.

"What book?" Her Grandpa looked at the sail and screwed up his eyes. He couldn't see what Rukmini could see. But she was so excited that he couldn't help feeling excited too.

"Tell me what it is! I'd like to see it too!"

"Oh Grandpa, the billowing sails are making a B. Look!"

"So they are!" he exclaimed. "I see it now—a big ballooning billowing, bouncing B!"

Rukmini hugged her grandpa. "This is a good beginning. I'm going to be a sailor like you one day."

"I think you will," her Grandpa said. "Just listen to the wind. It will teach you what you need to know."

* * *

In the evening on her way home, Rukmini stopped at Lauren's house. She knocked at the door and Lauren opened it. "I need to speak to you for just a second," Rukmini said. "My grandfather's waiting for me."

"Did you learn to sail?" Lauren asked excitedly.

"Yes, yes. But I need to borrow the book. Do you have it?"

"Yes, of course! Why? Did you find something?"

"I'll show you tomorrow."

"Okay," Lauren said. "Just a minute."

She ran to get the book for Rukmini who could smell that supper was ready at Lauren's house. She thought fondly of her own home and the smells of spicy dishes being cooked there for dinner. She'd forgotten all about the dark shadow beneath the waves.

"Here," Lauren said, appearing at the door. "Remember to bring it tomorrow. And the supplies."

"I'll remember. Thanks," she said, and hugged the book tightly.

* * *

Next day, as the sun slowly melted the mists away and Lauren and Sipho and Michael and Rukmini sat by their boat, Rukmini showed them the second page in the book.

"Here's the boat with the billowing sails, and there's me. I don't think I've ever done something like this. Look...a B! The billowing sails gave that to me...to us!"

"It's beautiful," Lauren said. "The sea almost looks enchanted. How did you draw that?"

"I don't know," Rukmini grinned. "It's just magic."

"That's two symbols!" Michael said. "Two letters, A and B. Are we ready to sail, to see what else we can find?"

"I have to tell you something. I'm very sorry, but I had to promise Grandpa that we'd stay in the bay and not go any further," Rukmini said. "Until we are all good sailors." She sighed impatiently, "We'll never get to the Wise Enchanter that way!"

The four friends thought for a moment.

"We could practice today," Lauren suggested. "You could show us what you've learned."

"We could all get good at sailing," Sipho agreed. "We won't have to stay in the bay forever!"

"Okay," decided Michael. "Let's all go and get good at sailing."

"I wanted to leave today," Rukmini sighed. "I know what to do."

"A promise is a promise," Sipho said. "We'll just practice today."

Rukmini sighed again, but all her friends agreed. And so that day they all learned the ways of the sea. Michael learned to tame the wind; Sipho learned how to tackle the dancing breezes; Rukmini began to understand the dark and light currents that swept beneath the boat, and Lauren became an expert at riding across the waves.

three

CLOUDS rushed across the sky and thunder rumbled in the distance. Lauren awoke to the sound of a branch scratching against her window. She rubbed the sleep from her eyes, stumbled out of bed, and went to look outside. Michael's face was peering up at her. He held a long branch that he was using to make a scratchy noise on the windowpane. Lauren stuck her head out. "What is it?"

"There's a big storm coming," Michael said. "We have to go and tie down the boat, and pull it further away from the sea."

Lauren dressed quickly and met Michael outside. The wind was blowing harder and fine raindrops were falling as the two friends made their way toward the beach. When they arrived, the sail was already billowing wildly. Michael had to use all his strength to tie it to the mast.

"We couldn't have sailed in this weather anyway," Lauren shouted over the crashing waves.

They pulled the boat up the beach as far from the pounding sea as they could. But they couldn't pull it all the way. They would have to leave it where it was, perched awkwardly on its side. The rain was closing in.

"The tide will come in too far," Lauren said. "We need to pull the boat back to the dunes. I'll stay here. You go and get the others."

"Okay," Michael said, and ran off to get help. Lauren tried to keep the boat upright, but a great gust of wind and the plink of a hailstone made her let go of the mast and run for shelter.

"Oh dear," she said, as she bent her head into the storm and ran to the Point of Rocks at the far end of the beach. She clambered up the jagged, slippery boulders, holding onto barnacled outcrops until she reached the top. The wide, flat expanse on top led along a high cliff. Lauren crept cautiously forward, crouching into the wind as she sought the shelter she believed she would find.

By the time Michael arrived at Sipho's house, hail was falling and whitening the ground.

"I left Lauren," Michael said to Sipho, his heart pounding. "Left her guarding the boat while I came for help."

"She might have run home by now," Sipho said. "She wouldn't stay out in the storm."

"I hope she did go home," Michael said. "But she didn't have much time. We have to go and look for her. Let's run to her house and see if she's there."

"Wait for the hail to stop. We don't want to have ice falling on our heads."

So they waited and watched, watched and waited. It was a long storm. Michael was sure Lauren must have gone home. Sipho thought so, too. When afternoon came the hail stopped. The sun sent a golden ray through the thick bank of clouds and the two boys made their way through the muddy puddles to Lauren's house.

But Lauren was not at home.

So this is how it happened that Lauren's mother and Sipho, Michael and Rukmini and some of their neighborhood friends went down to the beach in the early evening to find Lauren. There was no one on the beach. The boat lay safely on its side. The tide had not reached it. The sand glistened in the evening sun, hard and wet. Only the footprints of seagulls and herons could be seen. In the distance, the cliffs at the Point of Rocks plunged into the sea.

The group of friends, together with Lauren's mother, clambered up the jagged rocks. The sea crashed below them and showered them with droplets of spray.

"It's so high," said Rukmini with dismay. "Why would Lauren have come this way?"

No one said anything. Then after a while Sipho spoke quietly. "There are caves for hiding in, beyond the cliffs. I've seen them."

The sun went down, the waves turned to gold, and a rainbow spanned the dark clouds that were vanishing in the east. The group of rescuers came to the top of the cliff and walked along the flat, rocky ground. The first star came out and a thin crescent moon rose, but still there was no sign of Lauren.

The group carried flashlights and they shone them as the sky turned to a deep blanket of blue. Suddenly Michael gave a shout, "Look!"

By the light of the flashlights and the thin crescent moon, Lauren was clearly visible. She was crouching in a large sheltering cave-like overhang. The moon shone brighter.

"Here I am!" she shouted. Carefully climbing out, she gave a cry of relief and ran to hug her mother and her friends.

Overjoyed that his friend had been found, Sipho stared at the cave and the crescent moon. His eyes moved from one to the other and back again. Around him, everyone was talking excitedly. But he seemed to be in another world. Then he said to Lauren: "Look, Lauren. There was a reason why you got lost and we had to come and find you!"

Michael and Rukmini and Lauren looked intently at the cave, curving in the light of the crescent moon.

"It's a C. A clear, crisp, curly C. We must put that into our book!" Lauren exclaimed.

"I knew it!" Michael said excitedly. "There was a reason that we couldn't sail yet. Now that we have the C, we can go to sea!"

Everyone (Lauren included) was delighted that Lauren had been found. No one noticed the four children quietly singing: *See the C, See the C, sailing with the silvery C.*

They returned Lauren safely to her house, and everyone was invited to stay for supper, after which Rukmini ran home with Michael to get the Magic Book. Soon they were back at Lauren's house. The four children sat around in Lauren's room, laughing and talking. As they did so, Lauren worked carefully with her pencils. Before long, there was a beautiful new drawing in the Magic Book. "Look," she cried, "I can do it, too. This is like nothing I've ever drawn before!"

The children looked at the cave. The picture seemed to shine with its own light. Now each one of them knew that they could draw anything in the Magic Book and it would not be ordinary.

"We ought to say something before we leave tomorrow," Michael said softly.

"You mean, like leave a note?" Rukmini said. "So no one comes to look for us."

"And no one worries about us," Lauren added.

"Good idea," Sipho agreed. "We each leave a note and we meet at sunrise before anyone is awake."

That night the boat waited quietly under the bright starry skies for the day that lay ahead.

Four

DAWN stole softly across the bay. The children gathered around the boat to move it into the water. Lauren and Sipho pulled, Michael and Rukmini pushed, and eventually, after much pulling and pushing, the boat slid gently into the ocean without a sound. Into it they loaded many supplies, including the Magic Book, a compass, and a great deal of Courage. Lauren even took a beautiful precious stone, which had been a birthday gift from her mother. Then, without looking back, the four children hoisted their sail, and the boat skimmed gently away from the land.

The water sparkled. Rukmini checked for dark shadows, but there were none. She decided she must have dreamt the one she saw with her Grandpa. It was a beautiful, peaceful morning with just enough breeze to carry the boat swiftly across the water. They could see people on the shore beginning to arrive on the beach and set up their towels and umbrellas.

"My note mentioned that we'd be gone for about an hour," Michael said.

"This could be a very long hour," Rukmini said.

"This could be a very long hour," Rukmini said.

"Mine said not to worry, we're out learning in the bay for the morning," Lauren said.

Time, indeed, seemed almost to stand still.

After a while the breeze dropped and they began to sail into a dense, white fog. It was hard to tell whether they were moving or not. They dropped the sail. Suddenly, Michael, who was on the lookout, saw something. "Ship ahead!" he shouted excitedly. The others followed his finger and saw what he saw. Just up ahead was a snow-white ship, its prow, in the shape of a huge dragon, towering high into the mist. Slowly, their little boat—seeming smaller than ever—drew up alongside the huge dragon-ship. As it grew closer, they could see a stately old lady with pale skin and long, white hair at the helm. She waved and called to them.

"Children? Do I see children sailing the Sea of Silver?"

"Careful," Rukmini whispered to her friends. "She looks like a witch."

The old lady laughed when she heard Rukmini's words. "Oh no, my dears, you needn't fear me. I won't do you any harm. Not now."

"Who are you?" Michael called.

"Sail a little closer and I might tell you. I've come to warn you."

"Go closer," Sipho urged. "Let's listen to her. Remember? Listen to the words of old people."

"What if she isn't good?" Rukmini whispered.

"I'm not afraid," Lauren said. "Tell us," she called to the old woman in the dragon-ship. "We're here to listen. What's your name?"

"Ahh," she said. "My name is Dame Gothel. In my time I have been cruel and unforgiving. I was the keeper of Rapunzel many years ago. But I have learned humility. Now I am quite alone and lonely. I sail the Sea of Silver to warn travelers of danger. I see that you are on a difficult quest. I must warn you, Urckl is moving. His messengers are afoot. They are the devourers of light, of the words that lead to Wisdom. Be watchful of these waters, and of the islands you find. All is not as it might seem."

As she spoke the last words, the mist began to evaporate, and with it, the entire dragon-ship, until the four children rubbed their eyes and wondered whether they'd dreamed the whole thing. "Something's happened," Lauren said. "We seem to be in an enchanted place. What is Urckl?"

"I don't know," Michael said. The bottom of the boat scraped against sand and they ran aground. The mist had now dissipated completely. "Look, a dock on a little island. We can stop here for the night."

The island was small and rocky, with hills and dense underbrush. On every side, the Sea of Silver stretched out to the end of the world.

The children sailed in and tied their boat to a wooden pole. They climbed out onto the creaky dock and began to walk toward the mainland across a strange, pebbly beach. No one could stop thinking about the white dragon-ship.

That night the children slept deeply and without dreams. When they woke up, the sun was high in the sky. They rubbed their eyes and looked at their boat. The rope dragged loosely in the water. The dock had vanished. There wasn't a trace of it, not even a splinter of wood.

"The –ock's gone!" Rukmini cried.

"What shall we –o?" Lauren responded. And they all looked at each other.

"What's the matter?" Michael said. "You can't say your –ee's."

"You mean –ee's," Sipho added.

"Oh –ear," Rukmini sighed. "Maybe it's because of Urckl's messengers. Something's happening to our wor–s."

Michael got up. "Wait here," he said.

He walked away from the beach, toward the hill. Then he climbed up the hill and stood looking all around. He could see the wide glittering sea. He stamped his feet. He saw nothing, and nobody, and yet he knew that someone must have taken the dock! He cried out with all his might, "Whoever has taken the -ock, return what you've stolen!" and he stamped so hard on the hill that, all of a sudden, a door in the hill-side opened. A furious dwarf with a long beard stood before him.

"Who are you?" Michael asked, taking three steps back.

"I'm the dwarf of the door! What are you doing here? You're making a disastrous din!"

"Maybe you can help,' Michael frowned and looked past the dwarf into a huge chamber full of strange sights, that smelled of damp, torn earth.

"Don't want to,' the dwarf said. And then he yelled at something. "Don't! Don't!" Suddenly, Dachshunds came bounding out of the cave and vanished behind the hill. A diamond tumbled out onto the ground and then another, and Michael's eyes grew wide and round. Dragonflies exploded out of the rift in the hillside and landed on the dwarf's arm before they flew off into the light.

At his feet, a dormouse was trying to squeeze out into the bright sunlight. Michael suddenly felt pity for the creature, for as the dormouse inched its way out of the cave, the dwarf clearly meant to catch him. Michael leaned forward and grabbed the little creature by its front paws and pulled it into his arms. At that moment the dwarf flew into a rage. 'It's my dormouse!' he screamed as Michael tumbled backwards. All at once, the oddest collection of objects began to fly out of the cavern thick and fast behind the dwarf as he continued to shout, 'my dawn, my dock, my diamonds, my dormouse, mine, mine MINE!'

Michael turned and ran down to the beach, holding the dormouse as the peculiar collection came flying past him over his head. Finally he stumbled breathlessly onto the pebbly beach. His friends ran to him, calling out with joy: "The dock's back! Look! And what's that? What are you holding?"

Michael was so relieved to hear his friends speaking properly again, with D's, that he tried it himself. "This is a dormouse," he said softly and stroked it. "Rescued from the dwarf of the door."

To their amazement the dormouse began to speak in a very soft and furry voice.

"Thank you for rescuing me. You've rescued all the D's, you know. He was taking everything he could. He had orders. Everything was being captured—dogs, donuts, dancers, the dawn, the dusk. The D's were vanishing from the world, but you broke the spell."

"Is this something to do with Urckl?" Rukmini whispered to the dormouse, who put a paw to his lips.

"Shhh! Don't say it. He might hear us. It's time to go."

When they sailed away from the island of the dwarf of the door, they took the dormouse with them. He snuggled down at the front of the boat and, as the sun shone down on them and made the day beautiful, he slept, as dormice do. The children ate from their stock of supplies. Then Michael took out the Magic Book and began to draw as his friends watched. "The dwarf gave us a gift, even if he didn't mean to. We rescued the D's for our words, but look at how he's standing there with his hand on his hips. The dwarf is a D!"

When his three friends saw what he was drawing, they were full of joy. "We have the letter D," they said in one voice.

Five

EVENING came, and the wind dropped. The dormouse awoke and scuttled across the boat. "I'll keep watch at night," he said, sounding whiskery. "You sleep, and I'll be awake. That way, there'll always be someone to watch for shadows."

"What shadows?" Rukmini asked quietly.

"Oh, shadowy shadows," he said carelessly. "But probably I won't see anything. One messenger defeated already, so don't worry. Won't be anything for a long time. Where are we going anyway?"

"We're going to the end of the world to find the twenty-six symbols that will allow us to learn how to find the castle of the Wise Enchanter," Lauren said."

"Wise Enchanter, hmm..." The dormouse scratched his whiskers. "It's been a while, a very long while since any earth children came this way. I suppose it would be a good thing, if you could find him. We'd stop losing light, you know, if you found him. I'll come with you, help you all the way."

"Thank you, dormouse. What do you mean about losing light?" Michael asked.

"Oh, it's going dark. Very slowly, but it's going dark. It's a big cloud...it's...I can't say the name...*his* fault—he and his cronies like the dwarf. They're after the words of the world. There are fewer words used than ever before, haven't you noticed? No, no one notices, of course. No one speaks properly anymore. The words that aren't used at all anymore are devoured. Eaten up by something, see? Soon everyone will lose the ability to even tell a story, or say what they really feel. There simply won't be enough words. And another thing: people used to be able to understand animals. We humble creatures used to have a voice. Not now. Not anymore. No more talking animals except in stories or in the enchanted realms of a child's imagination. But that'll be gone too one day...all of us, devoured by the dark cloud of... Ignorance. Unless... hmm, well, you know."

"Is there anything more we can do now, to stop the cloud?" Sipho asked.

"Don't know," said the dormouse, twirling his whiskers. He thought for a while. "Well," he said finally, "I suppose it might be useful to find out about something that you didn't know before. Increase your Wisdom, so to say. Increase light, by a little, whenever you can."

Night came. The moon rose full over the Sea of Silver. The children and the dormouse ate. Then Sipho said, "I'll ask my ancestor for advice before I go to sleep. Perhaps he will give me a dream to help us."

That night, Sipho had a Big Dream. He didn't know what it meant, but when he awoke to the gently rocking boat he told his friends his dream:

"I was walking in the bushveld like I used to do before we left southern Africa. I looked at the big grey rocks behind the waving grass and went right past them to the shade of a msasa tree. When I turned, I saw that the rocks were not really rocks at all, but elephants. Hundreds of them. They were so silent that I didn't know I was surrounded, but I wasn't afraid. One of them walked over to me and draped his trunk around me, as if he were putting his arm over me. Then he walked to a tree, lifted his enormous body so that he was standing upright, and wrapped leaves and branches in his trunk to tear them off and eat. In the dream my ancestor said to me: *Remember the elephant, eh, who never forgets. Remember the silent elephant, eh, the silent E. The elephant is everywhere. If you carry him in your heart, eh, it will grow bigger and bigger until it is big enough to hold him. Understand, eh?* And then he laughed. *Eh, eh eh*, a big warm African laugh that made me homesick. Let me draw you the elephant, to show you how big he was, next to me."

"What does a msasa tree look like?" asked Michael. "Will you draw one for us?"

"Do elephants really remember?" asked Rukmini.

"I think they do," Sipho said. "Let me use a page in the Magic Book. I'll show you the big silent elephant, and the climbing one, and what a msasa tree looks like."

"And we'll all be wiser for it," said the dormouse sleepily through his two sharp front teeth.

Sipho drew for a long time. When he had finished, he was about to tear out the page, so that the Magic Book could be clean and new for the next symbol, but Rukmini put her hand over his to stop him. "Wait, she said. "Do you see what I see? The elephant looks just like an E! He's Enormous. His trunk is endless and makes an excellent E!"

Sipho looked at what he'd done. His friends smiled, and it seemed suddenly a little brighter, as if a small cloud had just moved away from the sun. The dormouse, who was lying at the front of the boat, sighed contentedly and turned around three times before finally finding a comfortable position in which to fall asleep. "Wiser for it," he muttered to himself. "Everyone, even me, a little wiser for it."

six

FOR many hours, the boat sailed the Sea of Silver. Nothing disturbed the glittering surface. Rukmini felt as if they were sailing over glass. It was so clear. You could see the world beneath the waves. Seaweed grew like waving grasses. Colorful fish swam between the corals and the rocks. Suddenly Rukmini longed to swim with the fish, to leap into the cool, blue world beneath the boat.

But just then the boat rocked sideways and a big swell surged up from the deep. The water grew cloudy as though something big had stirred up the sand. A shadow slipped by, followed by a shape so huge and dark, that Rukmini feared that something massive had crossed in front of the sun. The four friends looked at each other, and down at the depths. The shadow was below them. For a minute no one dared to take a breath. Then the shadow vanished ahead of them, moving away as swiftly as it had arrived.

"What is it?" Lauren asked, her voice barely a whisper.

Rukmini shook her head. "Don't know."

Whatever it was at the bottom of the ocean had disturbed the fish too, and now the fish leapt, or rather flew, exploding out of the water and plopping back in, as if someone were firing them rapidly out of a sea cannon. There were hundreds of them.

"Put up the sail!" Michael called. "Follow the flying fish!"

Michael and Sipho hoisted the sail and the wind caught it and blew them speedily after the fish. The fish continued to fly. They flipped and flopped, fins flapping, until Lauren and Rukmini and Sipho and Michael almost forgot their fear, watching the funny, frenzied forms darting in front of them. The dormouse slept.

The fish led them to a huge rock that jutted high out of the water. Bit by bit, they stopped flipping out of the water. Michael let go of the sail and it fluttered in the breeze. He shaded his eyes with his hands.

"There's something big and shiny flapping in the crevice of that rock," he said.

"Let's go closer and see what it is," Lauren suggested, joining Michael at the front of the boat.

Gradually, they came into the shade of the large rock. Every now and again a tiny fish, still frightened by whatever the big shadow had been, leapt out of the water in a shower of tiny droplets.

"Oh friends, it's a dolphin!" Rukmini cried. "A big bottlenose dolphin...and it looks like it's stuck!"

"I'll help!" Sipho cried, and took off his shirt.

"Me too," Michael said.

"We'll wait here," Lauren said.

The boys jumped over the edge of the boat into the sea and swam out toward the rock. Rukmini's heart pounded as she inspected the water for shadows.

"I don't feel as brave as that," she said quietly, as she watched the boys swimming toward the dolphin.

The dolphin flapped a fin. The boys arrived at the rock and climbed onto a small ledge next to the crevice. The dolphin was half in the water, half out, and it was clear it could not free itself from its rocky prison. The boys worked with all their might, gently, urgently, pushing and tugging and splashing the dolphin until at last, with a great whoosh, the dolphin was free, and it plunged down into the blue. Several fish burst out of the water, and Rukmini and Lauren felt tears of relief swelling behind their eyelids.

The boys slipped down into the water and began to swim back toward the boat. Suddenly, it was as if they were borne aloft. Something came up underneath them, and then they all saw that it was the injured dolphin. "Its going to carry us back." Sipho said. And he was right. The dolphin brought them safely back to their boat.

Rukmini held out her hand to help Michael, while Lauren helped Sipho climb back into the boat. The dolphin blew and snorted, bobbing its head out of the water. Then it swam beneath the boat and disappeared. The dormouse slept through everything. Nothing stirred him. All through the day, he stayed at the front of the boat, a perfectly round ball of soft fur.

"Do you think the dark shadow might have been chasing the dolphin?" Rukmini asked her friends.

"Yes," said Michael simply, and shook water from his hair. "I think the dolphin got chased into the crevice and wedged itself there by accident." Rukmini felt afraid. She knew now, beyond all doubt, that there was indeed a dark shadow and that it seemed to be following them. Suddenly she had the urge to escape and go home, really home—back to India, with the warm Indian Ocean just steps from her door and the smell of nan bread drifting from the house. But she knew she had much to do, and she tried to squash the uneasy feeling that rose up at the thought of the shadow.

"Do you think that could be the same dolphin we met at the beginning? The one who took us to the sea sprite?" Sipho asked suddenly. "It felt just the same when we were lifted up!"

"Maybe it was," said Rukmini, and she brightened at the thought.

"It felt as if this dolphin knew us, and trusted us to help," Michael said. Just then the children noticed all at the same time that the boat was touching sand. Ahead of them stretched a beautiful golden beach, shaded by coconut palm trees laden with fruit.

"We've hit land!" Lauren called laughing. "And just in time." The water was shallow enough for them to climb out of the boat and pull it to shore. "Wake up, dormouse," Lauren called to the sleeping bundle of fur in her arms. "Your night is over!"

"Hmm. So 'tis," he said slowly.

"I wonder what kind of island this is," Sipho said.

"Dolphin Island! Or Flying Fish island!" Rukmini pointed. "Look, everyone. Dolphins and fish everywhere!"

And there, in the bright afternoon sun, as the children gazed out to sea, they saw them: dolphins and flying fish, leaping for joy, flapping their fins in thanks. They swam backward and forward in front of the laughing children until the sun sank down to the sea, staining the rippling waters red and gold.

That night, by the light of a full round moon that shone on the beach, Rukmini opened the Magic Book. They all knew which letter they'd been given, and they watched Rukmini draw it. "Don't forget the flapping fins," Lauren insisted. Rukmini drew the picture perfectly: a fine set of fish and fins and a dolphin that looked like the letter F. Then she wrote a word in the sand, which all three of her friends could read. "We're learning to unlock secrets," she said. "We need to be...," and she wrote the word: "FED."

"Yes, we do!" They looked at the word in the sand and smiled at one another. Then they went back to the boat and pulled out their supplies for the night. They would have a good supper, or in the case of the dormouse, a jolly good breakfast.

seven

GADRUN hardly had the strength to pull herself out of the sea. Her tender skin was scratched and bruised, and her clothes were in tatters. Alarmed, the attendants from the castle saw her landing, and ran down to the water's edge to help her.

"Where have you been, your Majesty?" they asked, as they carried her to the castle. "Your father has been beside himself with worry."

"Apologize to him, please," Gadrun said. "I went to swim alongside four brave adventurers. I feared for them."

The attendants carried her up a steep, winding spiral staircase that ran around the outside of the castle almost to the top. It rose so high that the clouds touched the banisters with their hazy, white edges.

"I will take the message to your father," said one of the attendants. They entered the castle through a high, narrow door. Two women rushed to Gadrun's aid and set her down softly on her velvet bedcover. "Make sure you rest, now," they said.

"Thank you for your kindness," Gadrun whispered. She let her head sink down onto the pillow. Wind whipped through her open window and filled the heavy blue curtains. Then she slept.

When she opened her eyes her father stood at her bedside. His face was pale. Gadrun gently smiled at him. "It's all right now, dear father. I didn't mean to cause you worry. I felt compelled to follow our four friends for a while."

The Wise Enchanter frowned. His face was drawn and his voice had an edge of anger to it. "It has nothing to do with you whether these children succeed or not. You have no power over what will become of them or their journey. That's all entirely up to them. If they have the will, and the Wisdom, their quest will lead them in the right direction. If they falter, there is nothing either you or I can do. What are all these injuries you've suffered?"

"I leapt foolishly into a rocky crevice," she said. "I was rescued from my plight with great kindness. It would please you..." She looked away from her father. There was no more to say, but he'd seen the cold flash of fear in her eyes. "Don't worry, dear father," she tried to sound comforting. "I promise that I will be content now to wait with you. I have seen all I needed to see."

The Wise Enchanter could not be angry for long with his beautiful daughter. She had had no mother since the day she was born, and she had lost her love, a young Prince to whom she had been betrothed. One terrible windy day he had been captured and turned into a wild beast by one of Urckl's dark messengers. Though she had suffered greatly, Gadrun was still good and kind and true, with a heart as pure as her radiant countenance.

* * *

"It's colder here," Lauren remarked the next day. "It looks like it should be warm, but it feels like winter." A chilly wind pinched the children's cheeks and made them long for warm clothes. They found their jackets and gloves in the boat and dressed themselves warmly.

"I'll go and see if we can find a place to set up camp away from the water," Lauren said. "I was very cold last night." Tall trees called invitingly from the edge of the beach behind the coconut palms, and she was about to go, when Rukmini suddenly sat down on the sand and put her head in her hands.

"What's the matter?" Lauren asked, and ran to her friend. Sipho and Michael came running quickly too.

"I don't like this," Rukmini said, fighting back tears. "I want to go home!" She sniffed. "I miss my mother and my grandma and grandpa, and my cat Tickle. What if we never get to the castle of the Wise Enchanter? Maybe we'll never find him, and all this is for nothing. Maybe something horrible will devour us before we get there. Look what we've just seen...that...that dark shadow chasing the fish and the dolphin!"

Her three friends immediately came and sat down next to her. They all put their arms around her. "We'll make it," Lauren said softly. "Don't be sad. I miss home too, you know. I miss my mom and dad, and my silly pet goose Gilbert." She smiled at Rukmini. "Hey, let me tell you a Gilbert story. D'you know what he did on my birthday?"

"What?" Rukmini asked.

"I was so excited to be turning seven—especially because my mom gave me that gift I showed you at my birthday party—the blue gemstone, I forgot what it's called, the one that changes color with the light. I looked after that jewel all morning. I held it tightly in my hand. Then I put it on my dresser next to my bed and went out to play. But Gilbert is such a greedy guy! Once I was outside eating a sandwich and he just waddled up and grabbed the whole sandwich and gobbled it up!"

Rukmini laughed.

"At least I knew to keep food out of his way—but not other things. So I was playing outside, when I saw Gilbert snapping his beak together and trying to throw back his head to swallow something. Well, his beak made a funny noise. It sounded as though he had teeth and was chomping something. He made a noise like "Clack, clack clack." And then he said something that sounded like gaak, gaak gaak. I went up to him and grabbed him, and I saw that he did have something in his mouth, and it didn't look like something to eat. "Give me that," I said sternly. "Go on, Gilbert, give it to me." But he turned his head away. Then suddenly, he made a big noisy GAAAK, and out of his mouth came flying my precious gem. I picked it up and said, "Goodness gracious, me. Gilbert, gobbling gemstones is not what good geese should do! But thank you for giving it back." Gilbert was so embarrassed he looked away. I carried him to the pond and let him go and swim off his bad mood.

He's such a grumpy guy, but I miss him." Lauren said quietly, "I think we all miss our homes and our pets. But we're on an important quest, and we have to all be brave. Here, take the gemstone. I carry it around for good luck because it's my birthday stone. It helps me stay brave."

"It's beautiful," said Rukmini.

"Keep it for now." Lauren said. Rukmini opened her hand and Lauren placed the smooth, cold stone in her palm. "It'll help."

"Thanks," said Rukmini.

"Won't you draw Gilbert?" Sipho said.

"Okay," Lauren said. "While I draw you all rest. Then we can explore further." So Lauren went to get the Magic Book, and they sat there all together while Lauren drew Gilbert and the gemstone.

"I really don't like this island," Rukmini said, tilting her head to look at Lauren's picture. "Maybe we've lost our way. Anyway, I'm not giving up now. I want to go on with the quest."

"Great," Michael said. "And you know, you might feel better once we explore the island. If it is an island, that is. It seems kind of big. Who knows, we might find exactly what we're looking for."

They all turned their heads and took note of their surroundings. The dormouse, their night watchman, slept snugly on the beach with his back against the boat. Beyond the coconut palms, the forest continued to beckon. Sipho looked at the trees, and then once more down at the Magic Book. His friends watched as he traced the shape of Gilbert the goose, which Lauren had drawn, with his finger. "We might have already found exactly what we're looking for," he said softly. "Guess what Lauren, everyone. From the greedy gobbling goose, we have the letter G! We're not lost at all."

Lauren looked at her friends. Her eyes lit up with a sudden smile and she carefully shut the Magic Book. "Sometimes it feels like we're not doing anything at all and that the book is making this magic all by itself, don't you think?"

She wrapped the book in a cloth, and packed it into a bag. Then, gathering as many supplies as they could carry on their backs, in bags and over shoulders (including the sleeping, grumbling dormouse whom they bundled into a bag which Michael carried), the four friends made their way cautiously toward the forest.

eight

"HOW can we be sure that we'll find our way back to the boat?" Sipho asked. "The landscape is changing so quickly."

"I have the compass," Michael said. "We just have to retrace our steps when we've gone as far as we think we should."

Leaves crunched beneath their feet. There was a definite chill in the air, and as they made their way into the trees, they saw that it was fall, and that gold and red leaves lay spread out beneath their feet like a brilliant carpet.

Soon they were quite deep in the forest, and when they turned to look back, they could not tell from which direction they'd come. All around them trees stood like waving giants. Leaves rustled in the breeze and came spiraling down like a shower of amber and gold over the four children. Their noses were red with cold.

A branch snapped overhead and Michael looked up. And up. Everyone stopped and tilted back their heads to look at what Michael was looking at. There, high above their heads was a tree house, or a large platform fitted neatly between two tall strong trees. Right near the trunk of one of the supporting trees stood a long thin ladder.

"What was the noise? The crack?" Rukmini whispered.

"A squirrel or something, I think," Lauren said. Michael looked at his friends.

"We must go and see what's up there," he said.

"You first," Rukmini said.

Michael began to climb the ladder. Higher and higher he went until the ground looked far away. Reaching the top, he hoisted himself onto the platform. He almost fell down with surprise. For standing there, on a solid wooden wedge, against the trunk of the tree, with a beard as long as a foaming white river, a face as wise and withered as old bark, and eyes as deep as rock pools, stood a strange man. In his hands he held two giant walnuts, and he was cracking them in his palm.

"Oops," stuttered Michael. "I beg your pardon, sir. I didn't know anyone was up here." He looked over his shoulder at the ladder and began to make his way down.

The old man seemed not nearly as startled to see Michael. "Have no fear, boy. Stay and tell. Are you a real human boy?"

"Of course," said Michael, holding onto the sides of the ladder until his knuckles grew white.

"Yes, yes, of course you are. You look like a real boy. Do you know where you are, boy?"

"Um, not exactly."

"You have come far, far into the realm of the Enchanted Islands. I heard rumors, whispers on the wind that there were children coming, but it's been such a long time, such a very long time, that I doubted my own ears. This is good, boy. This is good. Are there more of you?"

"Three others. And an animal."

"Are they near?"

"Below the tree."

"Then fetch them up, boy. You can eat with me, if berries and nuts please you. I haven't had company in a hundred years. Go on! Fetch them up!"

So this is how it happened that Sipho, Rukmini, Michael and Lauren, (and the fast-asleep-dormouse who didn't), enjoyed a berry and nut feast with the Hermit who hid from the world in his high house.

"I left your world many years ago when I was young," said the Hermit. "I don't know how I left that world behind. It's hard to tell when one crosses from one world to another. But I knew I'd found my way through, just as you now have. And here I've stayed hidden from everyone, until now."

"Why are you hiding?" Lauren asked.

"I have no heart for the horrible racket, the heat and the crowds of your world. I abhor the noise — the noise with no words and no music. I had to find a place to hide. Tell me, children, are there any beautiful places left in your world? I heard they are fast disappearing."

"There are some," said Michael quietly, remembering to listen carefully. "Definitely, there are a few."

"Ah. That is good then. And why are you here?" asked the Hermit, but his eyes twinkled as though he didn't really need to know the answer.

The four children looked at one another. "We're trying to get to the castle of the Wise Enchanter," Michael said. "It's very difficult."

"But you have found your way to the Enchanted Islands. That is the first step, and that is good. I can't tell you which way to go, since I have no idea. You see, very few people have ever reached the castle itself, and no one has been there since I have been here, but I can tell you one thing. If you keep going straight through the forest, it will end. Just where it ends, there are two paths. One path is the Right Way. The other is the Left Way. One of these paths is the true way, and will take you where you need to go; but you can only know which is which once you have gone along the way of your choice for some time."

"Tell us, please!" they called out at once.

"What if the Right way is the wrong way, or the Left way is the right way?" Lauren asked. "It sounds confusing." The dormouse stirred, turning around in the bag as if he'd heard the conversation, but didn't wake up.

"Yes, yes, of course it does. But once you've done it, everything will be perfectly clear."

"And what about our boat?" Sipho asked. "We've left it on the beach. Will we find it again?"

"Not to worry, dear boy, not to worry," said the Hermit, and he smiled. "It will all be all right. Here, take some berries with you, and some nuts if you like. It's beginning to get colder. I'd hurry on if I were you."

"Thanks," Lauren said, and opened the bag with the Magic Book to make room for more supplies. The book tumbled out of its careful wrapping and fell open on the page with the G. The children gasped. A sudden gust of wind blew a whole lot of leaves across the page, and the Hermit reached down, picked up the book and blew the leaves from the pages, before carefully closing the book again and handing it to Lauren. "Thank you again," she said, and placed the book in the bag.

Michael hoisted the other bag with the sleeping dormouse onto his shoulders, and shook the Hermit's hand.

"Thank you, sir," he said politely.

The Hermit winked and watched as the children climbed down from his high house in the trees.

They continued walking through the forest until evening came, noticing that there were now fewer trees before them. The forest had begun to clear. But they were tired and found a circle of trees where they decided to rest for the night.

They unpacked the food, the blankets, and the dormouse, who seemed to have missed the entire day. Then Lauren took out the Magic Book because she meant to repack it carefully for the rest of the journey. As she opened it, a light breeze flipped the pages until the book lay open at the last picture. Lauren and Sipho and Rukmini and Michael and the dormouse were silent for several seconds. There, drawn by an unseen hand, was a picture of the Hermit hiding in his high house, talking to Michael. And as Michael looked at the picture of the house in the tree, he said quietly. "How did he do that? It's an H. A huge H. He helped us. This really is a Magic Book."

nine

IN the sunlit morning, the children saw that they had indeed slept at the very edge of the forest, and that they were, in fact, on the other side of the island, for the sea lay ahead again. It seemed to be much more blue than silver now, if it was the same sea, which no one could be sure of, since it looked completely different and everyone seemed to have lost all sense of direction. Two sandy pathways led through long grass toward the shore, and the pathways certainly didn't look very different from one another, and didn't look very much like important pathways either.

"Well, how are we to know which of these two paths is the correct one? They look exactly the same to me," Michael said.

"Right way, Left way, Light way, Wrong way. Anyway, Long way, hmmph," complained the dormouse tiredly, dusting sand from his front paws.

"So you weren't asleep all the time yesterday!" Rukmini said kindly. "You must be tired now. Why don't you climb into the bag?"

"I'll miss everything," said the dormouse. "Nothing happens at night. I'm keeping my eyes open."

"It feels right to go right." Rukmini said.

"Hands up those who think we should go right," said Michael. Three friends raised their hands. The dormouse blinked sleepily in the sunlight. "Okay, we agree then. Is that a paw in the air?"

"Nope," said the dormouse. "I'm scratching my head. I still think left."

"Sorry. Looks like you're out-voted," Sipho said. "Looks like we're going right."

"Whatever you say," yawned the dormouse. "But remember, I said left."

Rukmini held the dormouse and stroked his soft fur. "We'll wake you up if anything exciting happens. You can sleep now." But he wouldn't. So they walked along the short, sandy path until they came to the sea.

All at once, out of the water, a small green island arose. At first it was no larger than a stepping-stone, but it grew larger than that quite quickly. The island sprouted a growth that looked like a tree, and then something that looked like a bubble popped out of the top of the tree-like growth. First there was one, and then another, and another, and soon the whole sea was covered with strange, towering tree-islands; bubbles hovered over the islands in the air.

"What are they?" Lauren gasped.

"I don't know," Michael called back, and the next moment, he took a step forward, and jumped onto the first island. Then he leapt from the first to the second, while his friends looked on. "This is fun! Come on," he beckoned, and bounded to the next island.

"I don't like this one little bit," said the dormouse, nibbling on his words with his sharp little razor teeth. Before the children could pay much attention to him, something beautiful and colorful rose into the air from behind one of the bubbles. Then there was another of these, until the air was full of them.

"What's this now?" Rukmini whispered. "Butterflies?"

"Welcome to the Isles of Imagination," said one of the colorful things. "Let us inspire you. Here, anything that you imagine is possible. Whatever you imagine, you shall have. Your capacities here are infinitely interesting. All you need is an inkling of a wish and it shall be done. You may go wherever you imagine, traveling at the speed of thought. Imagine. Start with a place. Anywhere. Imagine where you'd like to be. Just say "I" and it is yours."

"I could just imagine that we're away from the island that we've just been on," said Rukmini. "That there are no islands anywhere in sight. I wish to be on solid, dry land."

"Think think think," sniffed the dormouse. "You might be missing something. A sort of look before you leap type of thing, I mean think. Look at the isles. Do you notice something eh? No, not the flying things. We've all seen and heard them." He scrambled out of Rukmini's arms. "You could be missing something. A symbol, maybe?" He said. "I knew there was a reason I didn't go to sleep. Get the Magic Book. Quick."

Rukmini scrambled around in one of the bags and found it, pulling it out.

"Now just draw what's in front of you," the dormouse said. His whiskers tickled Rukmini's fingers. "That's good: Michael standing on an island, and all the Isles of Imagination behind him. Good, good! Aha. I see it. I see it! I do! It's an I, an I!"

But Rukmini thought the dormouse was saying that he could see an eye. She didn't see any eyes. She blinked her own eyes and didn't even look at what she'd drawn. Then she hastily closed the book and distractedly picked up the dormouse who gave a furious coughing sneeze. Her friends were ahead of her by now, leaping from isle to isle, inspired and imaginatively impish. Rukmini followed the others, carefully stepping across the water, which seemed to be growing shallow and green.

ten

JUST a few moments later, the sea had turned miraculously into a bright green lawn and, when Rukmini turned to look behind her, the forest had completely vanished.

Cool fresh air blew across the grass, and the children ran. They ran and ran, stumbling and laughing at all the wide-open space in front of them. The rolling turf went on forever, until in the distance on a hill, the children spied a big blue structure with domes and turrets. It looked like it was made of glass. A little way down the lawn, something was bouncing up into the air like a large colorful grasshopper, and without knowing why, the children ran toward it.

"Where are we?" Lauren breathlessly asked her friends. "Is that a castle in the distance?"

"Doesn't really look like one!" Rukmini said. "But it's nice here." The dormouse, despite all the excitement, had fallen asleep in the bag.

Struggling against all their bags and supplies, they kept running. At last they came close enough to whatever was bouncing into the air to see what it was. And they could hardly believe their eyes. A jester in a colorful hat was jumping wildly up and down on a big round sunken trampoline. As they approached he whirled around. He had a kind, funny face. His eyes might have seemed sad for a moment, but he smiled any shadows away.

"Join me! Join me! I'm Jumping Jack. You first!" He pointed at Rukmini, and she stepped forward, putting her bag (and the dormouse) down on the ground. Jumping Jack the jester held out his hand. "Oh, joyful joy!" He shouted. "Children to play with! Come on, all of you. Jump with me! It's fun fun fun. Nothing but fun! Come and jump now everyone!"

Rukmini climbed up onto the trampoline. She jumped and laughed, and then her friends couldn't wait and they joined her. Soon they were all jumping and laughing and falling down, and Jumping Jack said: "Oh, we need more space for all of us. Come and play at my house, it's full of trampolines!" He jumped off the trampoline onto the grass. "Ouch," he said. "Watch the ground, it's hard." Then he turned, and with a light step he walked over to all their baggage and effortlessly picked up everything (including the dormouse in the bag) and danced onward across the green toward the big, glass structure on the hill. The children followed.

"Welcome home!" Jumping Jack said as they reached a magnificent rainbow-colored set of stairs that led up to the great blue glass domed house. He placed their luggage at the top of the stairs and the children stared in awe. When they stood on the first step, music began to play. They looked around in delight.

"Well, so you like my musical stairs! Good. We can play musical stairs (each stair plays a different instrument and many different songs) or you can join me in the jumping halls."

"Wait a second," Michael said. He ran up the stairs and down again, just to hear the sweet music they played. "This is great!" he said, and his eyes shone.

"Can we jump?" Sipho asked. "I'd like to see the jumping halls."

"Joy joy joy," Jumping Jack sang again and turned to open the massive doors that led into his house.

The inside of the house was astonishing. They entered a huge hall, but instead of a floor beneath their feet, the children found themselves standing on a massive turquoise trampoline. It rippled and shone like water.

"Jump!" said Jumping Jack. "As high and as far as you like."

The four friends jumped. They bounced so high they felt like they were flying. All across the great hall they leapt and laughed. They followed Jumping Jack down trampoline corridors and into more rooms with different colored floors that were all bouncy. The children were having so much fun that they could think of nothing else, except what was just around the next corner in the house.

When they could jump no more, Jumping Jack smiled. "I have so much room in my house," he said. "Stay as long as you like."

The children liked the Red Room the most, and decided to stay there, so Jumping Jack brought them their luggage and told them to join him for meals whenever they were hungry.

At sundown, the dormouse woke up. "What are we doing here?" he asked in a cross voice, and blinked his dreams away.

"Enjoying ourselves," Michael said. "Oh, dormouse, you should've seen us jumping. We've had so much fun."

"So that's what this is all about, hmmph? Fun?"

"Yes," Lauren laughed and lay back on the bouncy red floor of their room. "It's the most fun I've ever had in my life. It's all just joy!"

"Hmmph," said the dormouse. "Well, it doesn't look like you need anyone to be on guard tonight. I'll go exploring. Funny kind of floor," he said, testing it out. "Just like jelly. Wobbles when you walk. I don't know. Doesn't seem so much fun to me."

"It's all made out of trampoline stuff. Can you find your way around?"

"Course," said the dormouse. Lauren bounced herself comfortable and sent the dormouse by accident, flying out of the room.

The next day, Jumping Jack showed the children the rest of his house and his back yard. "Fun fun fun," he grinned excitedly. "Jump, joke, and have a jolly good time. No work, only play all night and day!"

They saw everything with amazement: in one room with high glass ceilings, stood a dazzling, pink indoor pool tiled with tiny rose-colored tiles. A pink canal led from the pool through an opening surrounded by glass to a vast blue outdoor pool. A rainbow fountain at the center of the pool glinted in the sun. From the pool, beautiful blue canals radiated outward through the grounds.

"It's no joke! You can follow the pink canals and swim right through the house," Jumping Jack said. "Then you can swim outside and all around the grounds by following the blue canals! Go on, be my guests."

Rukmini laughed and jumped up and down excitedly. "This is the best place in the world," she said. "I think we should stay here forever!"

No one knew how much time went by. The children swam and jumped and played and ate with the joyful Jumping Jack. They had forgotten about their boat, their dormouse, and even their journey.

And then one night, the dormouse arrived back in the Red Room, where the children were fast asleep after a very busy day of jumping and swimming, and he tried to wake them up. But his voice was too soft. The children tossed and turned and laughed in their sleep and made such a noise, that the dormouse was compelled to run from child to child, and give each of their toes a sharp little bite.

"Ouch!" Lauren woke up.

"Ouch, ouch!" Rukmini sat up.

"Ow!" Sipho was wide-awake.

"Oh that hurts!" Michael woke up. They rubbed the sleep from their very sleepy eyes and looked at the dormouse who blinked at them apologetically and sternly.

"What's the matter?" Rukmini asked, yawning.

"This," the dormouse whispered. His whiskery voice was no more than a hiss. "This is the matter! Can't you see? You've trapped yourselves here. There's no way out. I've been to the edge of this place and there's nothing but steep cliffs and gorges on either side, and a deep, cold river that runs through the bottom of the gorge. There's an icy wind blowing. The outside pool and all the blue canals have frozen over tonight. I smell snow, and darkness. So much for your inspired imaginations! Have you forgotten your boat? What about the journey? The Magic Book? Doesn't any of that matter anymore? Are you going to end your journey here?"

The children heard the dormouse as if he was talking from far away. His words took time to sink into their heads. Then they looked at each other, and each of them felt something like a heavy weight land in their hearts.

"Oh, dear dormouse," Rukmini said, suddenly wide awake, "how could we have been so thoughtless? What are we to do? Where is the Magic Book?"

The dormouse bounced to the door and from behind it, with his teeth, he grabbed the bag that had the Magic Book. "Open it," he said. "I've been busy in it, since you were engaged otherwise."

By now all four of the children were properly awake. They looked around and suddenly it didn't seem necessary at all to have such continuous fun.

They watched as the dormouse flipped the pages of the Magic Book. They came to the picture of the Hermit. "That's H," said Rukmini. "I don't remember what comes after that, though I know I drew it." She turned the page.

"The Isles of Imagination," Michael said. "I see them now, tall and straight, like I am. We almost missed it. I for *I am*, and *in* and *island* and *imagination*. And what did you draw, dear dormouse, that we might learn from you?"

The dormouse turned the page yet again. "It's him! Jolly, jovial, joyful Mr. Jumping Jack. You did it dormouse! It's a J!" Lauren said. "We would've missed that one too. Oh, thank you, dormouse. We have it now and, most importantly, we've remembered what we're doing. We must leave here immediately."

And so, under cover of darkness, and to the great relief of the dormouse, the children left the house of Jumping Jack. Outside it was cold and they shivered. Lauren carried the dormouse and Sipho led the way because his eyes were sharp in the night. He'd grown up in Africa under ink-dark skies and could see things that the others couldn't.

Quietly and with careful steps, they walked to where the undulating land plunged down steep cliffs into rocky gorges.

"Can you see anything on the other side?" Michael asked, as Sipho stood precariously at the edge of a smooth granite rock and blinked in the darkness.

eleven

"KIND OF," he said. "The gorge is deep, but on the other side it looks like the land continues. If only there was a bridge—it wouldn't be very far across at all."

"Been around the whole place twice," said the dormouse. There's no way across, and as far as I can see, there's no way down. And if we got down, we'd have to swim."

The children peered into the darkness in front of them. The air was cold and bit into them. Then Rukmini said quietly: "If we got here by traveling across the Isles of Imagination, then...."

"Then what?" asked Lauren.

"Then surely there is a way for us to get out of here. We just have to use our imaginations. The dormouse is right, we are the ones who trapped ourselves here, and we're the only ones who can get ourselves out. I'm going to close my eyes and imagine something other than Jumping Jack." Rukmini closed her eyes. Then she opened one eye and looked around, and looked at each one of her friends. No one said anything for a while.

"I don't think it's working," Michael sighed. "It's late. We're stuck here. What are we going to do?"

"In the day you might be able to see better," said the dormouse kindly. "You can rest here and I'll watch and listen. When Jumping Jack discovers you've gone he's going to be jolly upset."

"After all his kindness, it seems rude to leave like this."

"It's the only way," said the dormouse sternly. "You'd never get away otherwise. He'd have you all excited about some new joy-toy and you'd stay there forever. Believe me."

Rukmini stroked the dormouse's soft fur and sat down on the grass. They all sat down and huddled close to keep warm. Rukmini yawned and said: "I think, maybe, when we chose the pathway, we chose the wrong one. We should have listened to the dormouse and gone left. It might have been so much better that way."

"Oh, tut tut. No regrets. I'll wake you up at sunrise," the dormouse said. The children, who'd been tired anyway, and had then had to wake up and escape, didn't need any more encouragement. They leaned on each other and promptly fell asleep.

A loud birdcall woke Sipho first and then Lauren. The dormouse was up on his hind legs sniffing the air. Rukmini and Michael stirred and sat up. They glanced in the direction of the noise and narrowed their eyes against the blinding rays of the morning sun. There was movement on the opposite side of the gorge.

Someone was walking toward them waving both arms. He called out at the top of his lungs, "Good morning!"

"It's not a bird," whispered Sipho to Michael. "We weren't woken by a birdcall."

"Suppose not," Michael agreed.

"Good morning!" called Lauren and Rukmini in one voice. The figure came closer. When he arrived at the edge of the cliff on the other side of the gorge, the children were astonished at what they saw.

The waving figure was a king. He was dressed all in purple, and his heavy gold crown caught the rays of morning sun and shone so brightly that it was difficult to look at him. "Good morning!" he called out again. "What are you doing over there?"

"Oh, your Majesty! Is there a way across?" Rukmini asked.

"Why, of course, my dear."

"Oh! That's wonderful. Where is it?"

"It's right here in front of you."

Rukmini looked from the King's quiet countenance to the gaping gorge in front of her.

"I don't see anything," Rukmini replied distrustfully. She searched the King's face to see if he was perhaps making fun of her, but she saw only kindness in his eyes.

"How...how do we get across?"

"Good question. The answer is, you walk—one foot in front of the other."

"We can't walk on fresh air!" Rukmini pointed out.

The king took out three golden balls and began to juggle with them. "Yes you can," he said, concentrating on what he was doing. "Trust me."

"Why?" Rukmini asked.

"Because I am the kindest king, and because, as you might know, since time began, all true heroes have to learn trust, and it is only with trust the answer comes. You take a step in faith, and something catches you."

"What if I don't have any trust, and I take a step without it?"

"Once you take a step, you have trust. The words hold true. Try it."

Rukmini noticed her friends looking at her expectantly. "Try it," Michael whispered. "Just think of yourself walking across, and us following you."

"I believe him," whispered the dormouse.

So Rukmini went to the edge of the gorge. She took one last, long look at the king who winked encouragement. Then she closed her eyes and put her foot out into pure fresh air, and when she opened her eyes, lo and behold, beneath her feet was a solid little wooden bridge, which spanned the entire gorge.

Rukmini, followed by Michael and Sipho, Lauren and the dormouse, walked across the bridge, which swayed very gently. And then they were safely on the other side.

"Thank you!" Rukmini said, and curtsied in front of the King. "You've saved us."

"No. You did it on your own. Without your own courage nothing like this could be accomplished. I wish you luck wherever you might be going."

"What will we find if we go north?" Michael asked.

"The Whispering Woods. You should find plenty to eat on the fruit trees there. Just remember to stick together. It's easy to get lost. Goodbye, my friends."

When the Kind King left them, the children sat down on the ground and took out the Magic Book. They all knew exactly what his Majesty had given them. While Michael drew the others all added their comments. "His crown was bigger," said Rukmini.

"He stood royally," said Lauren.

"Look at him now," said Michael. "The Kind King has given us the letter K."

twelve

LATER that morning the children were walking among tall oak trees. The sun was almost in the middle of the sky. Gone were the Kind King, the rolling green lawn, and the steep, rocky gorges. The air seemed to have lost its chill. The children found a shady place at the foot of a giant oak tree and spread out a cloth and some food. They had not eaten anything since the night before and all of them were hungry. And there were indeed fruit trees—apple trees, to be exact. Sipho climbed up to the high branches to get the best ones.

Somewhere in the woods they could hear a stream gurgling.

"I'll go and get water," Michael said. "I won't be long." He took a small flask and waved to his friends. Then he set off through the Whispering Woods to find the stream that sounded so near.

Michael hadn't gone very far when he came to a clearing. In the middle of the clearing was a small, blue lake, fed by a crystal clear stream that chattered and danced over pebbles on its way to a pond. The wind whispered through the branches, and it sounded as though the leaves and trees were trying to tell him something. He strained to hear what sounds they were making, but his ears could only hear the breeze.

Michael walked around the edge of the blue lake, which reflected the bright clouds in its smooth surface. When he came to where the stream fed into the pond, he knelt down and dipped his flask into the fresh cold water.

No sooner had he done so than there was a ripple in the lake and a beautiful girl emerged from the water. A strange glow surrounded her. Michael dropped his flask, and it sank to the bottom of the lake. The girl came out of the lake, smiled lightly at Michael, and then knelt on the ground near him and looked at him. "Hello," she said and stretched out her hand. "I'm Lilah of the Lake."

"Pleased to meet you," Michael said and took her cold hand in his. "I'm Michael. Do you live near here?"

She had a lovely laugh. It tinkled and rippled like a bubbling stream. "No, no. You saw me! I live in the lake, silly. I live in the water. Under the water, if you like. I notice you dropped your flask. If you'd like me to show you where I live you could follow me, and we could get your flask back." She smiled at him so sweetly that Michael wanted nothing more than to go where she would lead him and look and look at her lovely face.

"Okay," he said haltingly. "But I don't think I can go very deep. I don't live under water and I can't breathe there." He thought briefly of his friends, waiting for water. Then he looked at Lilah and her laugh chased away all his cares.

"Leave that all to me," Lilah said. "I'd be delighted to show you where I live. Come on!"

He took her cold hand again, and she got up and led him slowly into the water. When the lake was up to his waist, he paused and looked around. For a moment he felt alarmed. But Lilah turned to him and looked at him with such love that he followed her deeper into the blue. He began to notice that they were simply climbing down stairs, and as his head went under the water, the light merely changed, so that he seemed to be walking in a meadow where dappled sunlight glimmered through the branches of a tree. "Isn't it lovely?" Lilah exclaimed. "Look, I have a meadow of lake weed, and my fish fly through the water just as birds fly through the air!" She reached out her hand and took hold of an eel as it sailed by, wrapping it around her wrist. "This is my pet Lulu," Lilah said. Michael didn't like the look of Lulu very much. She had a fierce, sulky mouth and glassy eyes. Michael let go of Lilah's hand. She bent down. "Well, here's your flask." She said, "Would you like it?"

"Thank you," said Michael and took it.

"So," Lilah said, and turned to smile at Michael. He felt his heart would break if she stopped smiling. "Do you like it here?" She asked. "You can live with me forever you know. I'd love to have you down here. I've been longing for a friend, for someone to play with. I lured you here with the whispering rush of the stream. I knew you were thirsty, and I saw you and your friends and I liked you. I thought you'd be the one to like it underwater. Do you like it here? Say you do!" And when she said that, tears filled her pretty big eyes and rolled slowly down her cheeks. Michael wanted to stay and stop her crying, and be her friend, but he suddenly thought of his three friends waiting for him. He felt as though the water had crept into his head and was making his thinking soggy.

"I kind of like it here, Lilah, I never knew that it could be lovely under the lake, and... yes, I might like to be your friend. But... you see, I have friends who need me, and I need them, and we're on a quest, so I really should be getting back to them. I think I'd miss my life above the water very much. So, thanks for the flask, I'll need that, but I suppose I'd better be getting back now."

All at once Michael was afraid that if Lilah wept any more, he would never be able to leave her, so he turned his back on her, and began to leap through the water, toward the stairs and the shallows where he'd first come in. Behind him he heard Lilah cry out, "Don't leave me! Please don't leave! Your friends have each other. I'm all alone and lonely. Oh please don't leave!"

But Michael's head was already out of the water. He took a great gasp of real air and dragged himself out of the lake. For a moment he lay exhausted on the sand. Then he picked up the flask, which was full of water, and ran through the Whispering Woods to where his three faithful friends were waiting.

"What took you so long?" Lauren asked, and Michael could see that she had been worried.

"We were starting to think you were lost," Rukmini said. "The trees had begun to whisper things that sounded like *look, he's lost*."

"I wasn't lost," Michael said. "But I almost was. Let's get the Magic Book. I'll show you what happened."

So while they drank thirstily from the flask and ate bread and nuts and fruit from their supplies and from the generous trees, Michael drew, and as he drew, he talked. "This is lovely Lilah of the lake who lives deep under the water. She lured me down into her world and wanted me to live there and not come back. I almost couldn't leave, and when I did, she cried."

"You had to leave," Sipho said and patted his friend on the back. "But don't feel sad. Look at Lilah," Sipho said. "She's kneeling just like a large L."

"She is! Though I had to leave, she's still here in this picture, and she can live on with us in many words that we write and speak! I wish she could feel this: I haven't left Lovely Lilah all alone. She's with us for always. She's a lovely, lovely L."

thirteen

MICHAEL was the first to notice how the landscape was changing as they walked. The trees thinned out until the Whispering Woods were gone, and the ground became hard and arid. In the distance beyond dusty hills and mounds loomed a magnificent mountain range.

"It looks like India," Rukmini said.

"No. It's like Scotland," Lauren said.

"It's like America, for sure," Michael said.

"It's definitely more like Africa than anything I've seen," said Sipho. When they stared at the mountains in the distance, the children felt like they each knew the mountains from some long-forgotten time, and they walked faster to reach the foothills, as though they were expecting to find something there.

After a while, a little white goat wandered out of nowhere into their midst.

"A mountain goat!" Sipho said. "This must be Africa."

"Meehh," said the goat. "Meeh."

The dormouse poked his head out of the bag, where everyone believed he was fast asleep. "Nope. He's not one of the talking animals. Let's move on."

But the goat went up to Sipho, grabbed Sipho's clothes in his mouth, and pulled him toward a mound of earth. And there he began to bleat until Sipho held out his hands to the goat and spoke. "What is it, little goat? You may not be a talking animal, but what do you want to show me?"

"Meh, meh," said the goat, and jerked its head in the direction of the mound. "He wants me to see something," Sipho said, and went where the goat pulled him. Then he knelt down in front of the goat and held out his hand. The goat pushed his hand with its nose until it was pointing at the mound.

All the children noticed the mound at once. They saw it because it moved. And when they looked at it more directly, they saw that it looked amazingly like a giant pair of lips, and that the mountains in the distance looked like a giant nose and giant sleeping eyes. And the giant lips were indeed moving, because they spoke.

"Mmmm," said the huge mouth, and the sound was like the deep, satisfied rumbling and mumbling of earth and rocks. The ground seemed to tremble beneath the children's feet. When they looked around, the goat had wandered off. "Many moons have gone by since any children have made such a journey. You know this. Most of the time no one makes it as far as the Enchanted Islands. Now you have come far—right inside the Isles of Imagination. Mmmm. May my words go deep into all your hearts. I am the Mountain, the Mountain of all Mountains. I must mention the monster. His name I cannot name, but the warmth and light in the world is fading. When you require courage, look into your Magic Book. I have made myself there, and I will warm you, so that deep in your hearts you may feel my might. Take the might of mountains and make it your own and you will feel immense. Hold tight to the magic gemstone. It means more than you know." As the mountain spoke the last words, it seemed to breathe a sigh, which became a gust of wind so strong that it blew the children over. The earth rumbled and shook, and great cracks appeared. Out of two enormous cracks, two tall trees grew. The children stumbled toward the trees as huge clouds rolled in overhead and it began to rain. It rained so hard that the children could see almost nothing, and then just as suddenly as the rain had appeared, it stopped. A bright rainbow shone in the sky. The dry ground had turned to mud with new shoots of green grass poking through it.

"Open the Magic Book," Michael said. Sipho unpacked it and unwrapped it, and they all bent over to see what the Mountain had magically made.

And there he was, the Mountain with the mouth, and the distinctive shape of the mountains in the distance. "Mmmm," Sipho said. Magnificent courage spread through all their hearts, making them all feel warm inside.

"The Mountain's mouth is like a small M." Lauren said. "And the mountains in the distance are a marvelously large M. It must be magic. Oh, Rukmini, do you know where my gemstone is? We mustn't lose it. The Mountain said so."

fourteen

"NO! I can't seem to find the gemstone," Rukmini said, fumbling in her pockets. "I know I had it. I did! It gave me courage when we were leaping across the Isles...dear me, what if it fell out while I was leaping across the sea? Oh, Lauren, I'm so sorry!"

"I'm certain it's somewhere. Don't worry. Maybe it'll turn up in a bag. It's okay. I'm sure we'll find it again."

Rukmini felt very bad indeed. The Mountain had to have mentioned the gemstone for a reason. Now she couldn't find it and she was sure it had fallen out of her pocket into the sea when she was jumping across the Isles of Imagination. "I think we definitely chose the wrong path," Rukmini said.

"I don't think so," Michael said gently. "Had we taken the wrong path, we would have had no more letters for our Magic Book. Who knows, maybe there is no Right Way or Wrong Way. Remember that the Hermit said there was a Right Way and a Left Way. He said one of the ways was the true way. But he didn't ever say that one of the ways was the wrong way, did he?"

Rukmini shook her head slowly.

"So, maybe the way that we choose becomes the true way, because we choose it, and maybe there is no wrong way!"

Rukmini thought for a minute. "I think you're right," she said slowly, understanding what Michael had understood. The others nodded their heads.

Night fell gently around the four children. The few blades of grass that had poked up through the mud in the rain turned into a juicy pasture. The stars came out and the wind that blew was not as cold as it had been when they left the house of Jumping Jack.

"I think I actually smell the sea," Rukmini said, and all three of her friends took deep breaths.

"I do, too," Sipho said.

"We can probably sleep here tonight," Michael offered.

"I'm not sure I really want to find the sea," Rukmini said. "It reminds me of that shadow." They all looked up as, one by one, the stars came out. The dormouse was wide-awake now, scuttling around and making sure that the surroundings were clear. The children lay on their backs on grass beneath the night that was so dark that the stars coming out seemed close enough to touch. Soon the whole deep blue dome of sky was filled with a billion brilliant stars—gems that filled the children's hearts with awe as they drifted off to sleep.

Some time during the night Rukmini awoke. She could hear the dormouse gently nibbling on a nut. As she looked up at the sky, her heart pounded with delight. It seemed as though she were deep in the sky herself. She could actually see the planets. She could see that one of the planets had a shimmery ring around it. Once her uncle had allowed her to look through his giant telescope, and she had seen the ringed planet and a beautiful pink and blue cloud that her uncle had called a nebula. "What is that?" she'd asked him. His answer had been, "star dust, or star gas, my dear girl." Now, as she looked at the heavens so close to her, she saw the same thing again. A huge blue and pink and purple cloud in a shape, sprinkled with little twinkly stars that swooped up and down and up again, filled the darkness above her head.

"A nebula in the night," Rukmini whispered. "It's the nicest thing I've ever seen." And then, to her amazement, she saw little beings diving around the sky. At first she thought they were shooting stars, but the longer she looked, she saw that they had heads, tiny little faces, and arms. Their bodies seemed to dissolve in light.

"What are you?" she whispered in delight, not expecting an answer.

"We are the nixies of the night," one said, and shot upward toward the nebula and then came down again.

"Why is everything in this night so near?" Rukmini asked.

"Things are much nearer than you think," the nixie of the night said. "It's the people who are usually so far away."

"Oh," said Rukmini. "Can you tell me what this nebula really is?"

"Yes," said the nixie of the night. "The nebula is a halo of light that Mother Nature places around the most ancient of stars, because when stars grow ancient, they are allowed to begin giving their light to the new little stars being born. Mother Nature helps them. Can you see the new little stars in the halo of light?"

"Yes!" Rukmini exclaimed, but her eyes were growing very tired. The nebula was so bright she wished she could stare at it forever. Eventually, however, without her noticing, she fell asleep. Some hours later, the bright morning rays of sun on her eyelids woke her up.

The first thing Rukmini did was shake the dozy dormouse. "Dormouse!" she said excitedly. "Did you see anything last night?"

"Nope. Nothing much. Well, I spotted A-nowl," he yawned, "an owl, a spotted owl to be exact. And I heard a night warbler."

"What about the stars—the night nixies and the nebula?"

"Nope. Not a thing, I'm afraid. A most uneventful night, thankfully."

Michael and Sipho and Lauren slowly woke up. "What were you saying?" they asked, blinking their eyes against the bright morning sun.

Rukmini fumbled in the bag for the Magic Book. "I know this wasn't a dream. It didn't feel like one. This is what I saw last night." And she began to draw. "These are the nixies of the night. And this is a nebula. A nixie of the night said that the nebula is a halo of light that Mother Nature places around ancient stars. The ancient stars give this light to their baby stars, which are being born. I know this nebula is not just a nebula. It's a gift from Mother Nature."

"That's not all." Lauren exclaimed. "It's also an N! N is the fourteenth symbol; it's the fourteenth letter of the alphabet."

"Well," said Sipho. "Now we know. We can't give up, even if we have to brave the open sea and its dark shadow again. We're getting closer. Now I know we *have* to do it."

The four children packed away their book, packed up all their things, and as the sun rose higher into the sky, walked through the damp grass toward the smell of the sea.

Fifteen

"OH, I see it!" Sipho called out. "It looks like the Sea of Silver again!"

"It does!" Lauren agreed. "But how can we ever find our boat again? The beach doesn't look anything like the one where we came to shore after rescuing the dolphin. We've come such a long way since then. I don't know where we are."

"The Hermit told us that it would be all right. We should trust him," Michael said.

"But old Dame Gothel on the dragon-ship told us to be watchful of all these islands," Rukmini reminded her friends. "And I haven't found the gemstone," she added sadly.

"At least, we can be watchful and have trust," Lauren said. "Let's go down to the beach."

They reached the beach and took deep breaths of sea air. Tiny sandpipers ran along the shore, while seagulls dipped into the waves and soared up into the air again. Lauren walked a little way away from the others to see what lay beyond the curve of the beach. As she walked, the wind blew stronger. The sun was still bright, but patches of morning fog and mist still hung over the sea.Below them, the sea spread out like a silvery blue carpet. Little waves lapped at the golden shore. The children had grown accustomed to the changing weather, which was sometimes kind and then, quite unexpectedly, so bitterly chilly that they would have to pull out their scarves and sweaters. For now, the air was gentle and a little cool.

Suddenly, a gust of wind stopped Lauren in her tracks. She had been about to step in a puddle of seawater when she looked up. Before her, in a swirling mass of fog and sea spray, Lauren saw an exquisite face. Then she saw that the swirling fog was really hair, and that the shimmering puddle before her was part of a dress. The beautiful being held something in her hands. Her arms and hands sheltered whatever she held as though she was carrying it very carefully.

"Oh," Lauren gasped. "What are you?"

There was laughter like the rushing of the tide over thousands of shells.

"I am Opal," said the being. "I'm returning to you what was lost."

"Oh," Lauren said again, as the being held out her iridescent, almost transparent hand. Lauren looked in astonishment. Lying in Opal's palm was her lost, precious birthday gemstone.

"This is yours, this opal. I could see your picture in it. It told me where to find you."

Lauren remembered the name of her precious stone. It was, indeed, an opal.

"Thank you, thank you!" she exclaimed. "I knew I'd see it again."

The bright being Opal stretched out her hand and placed the opal into Lauren's waiting hands. "This is no ordinary opal," she said. "It was a birthday gift, full of love, given to you by someone older in your family. It is your birthstone for the month of October. If you ever need to know something, look into the opal and it will reflect what you need to see. Even the future may be revealed in its translucent blue depths.

Hold it to your ear and you will hear the whispers of Wisdom from the ancient ones, for opal has been upon the earth since time began and has known the earth since then."

Lauren clasped her gemstone tightly in her hand and gazed at its beautiful blue color. "I don't know how to thank you...."

When she looked up, only a small wisp of mist hovered above the sand. The bright-faced Opal had vanished into the light.

Lauren ran as fast as her legs would carry her back across the sand. "Look, everyone, look!" she cried, quite out of breath. Her friends came running towards her. "I've got my opal, my gemstone! I have it back!"

"Oh, look, she does have it!" Rukmini shouted with delight. "Where did you find it?"

"Was it in your pocket?" Michael asked.

"Oh, no," Lauren said, and took a deep breath. "It was really lost. And now it's really back again—thanks to Opal—and it's really a magic stone and I'm really going to look after it now."

They all sat in the sand. Lauren had the Magic Book on her lap and everyone watched while she drew the beautiful Opal holding the precious stone. "Oh!" Everyone said in one voice. The drawing grew more and more brilliant before their eyes.

"Yes!" Lauren said, and looked with bright, smiling eyes at her three friends. "Here is O. Opal gave us the letter O. The real stone is zipped tightly into my shirt pocket. If we need it, I can get it."

She closed the Magic Book carefully and wrapped it up to pack away. "The Book is definitely getting heavy," she said.

"Now we should walk. Let's follow the curve of the sea and see where the beach goes, and see whether we recognize anything," Michael said.

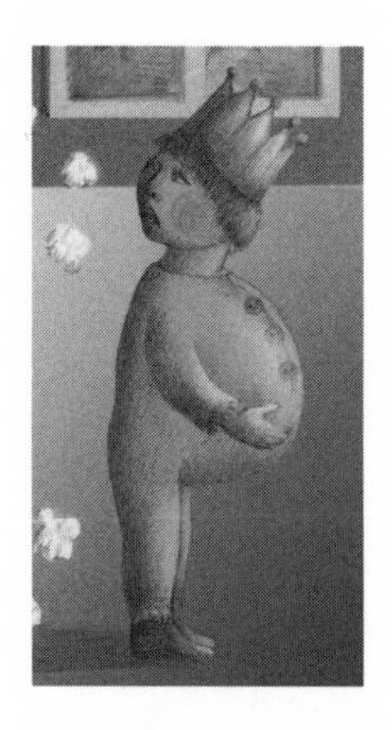

sixteen

PELICANS plummeted out of the sky, plunging down into the sea as they chased after their meals. The children followed the coastline for several hours but still did not see anything familiar. Now it was afternoon and the hot sun made the children weary. The sand shimmered in the haze and they were about to stop for a rest, when they looked ahead.

Each of them rubbed their eyes, for it was hard to believe what stood there in the sand.

"A purple palace?" Michael frowned.

It was true. A purple palace indeed rose up out of the wide sands. There was nothing else around the palace, and its doors stood wide open, inviting anyone in.

"Who would be living here?" Rukmini asked.

"Let's go and find out," said Michael, who, although he was tired, suddenly found the energy to race ahead. His friends followed more cautiously. When he arrived at the wide-open purple door, he went in. He stepped onto a cool, tiled floor and looked around. Everything inside the palace was purple—the floors, the walls, the ceilings. Even the pillars were made of purple stone. Rukmini and Lauren and Sipho stepped inside the palace. "I wonder who lives here," Lauren said.

"Could be...that the Urckl thing lives here," Rukmini whispered fearfully.

"Shhh," Sipho said. "I don't think so. It looks so empty. It's as if nothing lives here."

The children began to explore. They slid along the slippery floors and ran their hands along the smooth, cool walls. Eventually Michael came to a tall pillar. Beneath the pillar, there was a purple pot. Michael lifted the pot and all at once, a popping sound filled the air. The children stood as still as statues for a moment until they realized where the popping sound was coming from.

"The purple pillar is popping purple popcorn," Michael exclaimed. He moved the pot so that it would catch the popping popcorn.

"Do you think it's all right to eat?" Lauren asked. "I'm so hungry."

Michael took a handful and popped it into his mouth. He closed his eyes and crunched it. "Delicious," he pronounced. "It's just purple popcorn. Come on, everyone. Let's eat!"

So everyone took their turn popping purple popcorn from the pot into their mouths. They enjoyed it enormously. It was deliciously salty and warm, and they were much hungrier than they had led one another to believe.

All at once a door slammed.

The children jumped, it was so loud.

"How dare you eat my popcorn?" yelled a furious voice.

They turned to see who it was. At the far end of the hall, stood a plump little prince. He was dressed all in purple, except for his crown, which was made of pure, heavy gold. He patted his round stomach nervously with his fingers, and his face was purple with rage.

"Apologize this instant," he said. "And who are you anyway? I'm supposed to be here by myself!"

Michael wiped the salt from his lips and walked to the prince. "Apologies, your Majesty," he said politely. "We really had no idea that anyone lived here."

"I don't live here," said the prince promptly. "I've been *put* here. And I can't escape either, because the sea is truly perilous."

"What do you mean?" asked Rukmini, coming over to stand in front of the purple prince. The prince looked from Michael to Rukmini, to Lauren, to Sipho.

"The sea is perilous, because of a dreadful sea monster, if you please. A perfectly horrible thing," he said. "I know I only saw the tail, but it was as long as a ship. And I have been *put* here, for *pouting*, of course! My dear Papa kept saying to me that if I didn't stop pouting and do something useful for someone for a change, I'd find myself all alone on an island, with no friends at all. And one day, after a pouting until my lips were purple, because Papa wouldn't pop me popcorn to please me…poof! My whole house was gone, and Papa was gone too, and here I was. And I guess I get to stay here until I stop pouting. I have all the popcorn I could want, but I'm still pouting because there's nothing I can do for anyone anyway. I'm entirely useless," he said peskily. "And I don't care."

The plump prince pushed his gold crown down on his head. "I suppose I don't mind if you help yourself to popcorn," he added. "Plus, you might tell me what you're doing here. Did you also make your Papas angry and find yourself in this predicament?"

Rukmini's heart had begun to pound at the mention of the monster. She believed without a doubt that this was the shadow they'd seen beneath the waves from the very beginning.

"Thanks for the popcorn," Michael said. "And goodness, no, we're not here for that reason. We got here by accident like you. The Isles of Imagination led us here. Perhaps your imagination just happened to lead you to the same spot. But we're on a journey. A very serious quest."

"I see. But would you all like to stay for a while, and play in my purple palace?"

"Thank you, but no. We have to go, really we do," Lauren said, remembering Jumping Jack and how much fun they had had in his jovial presence, and how distracted they had been so that they'd almost entirely forgotten the purpose of their journey.

The prince's bottom lip stuck out and he held his breath until his face was purple with disappointment. He pouted furiously while the children stared and stared at him, and wished he would stop pouting and find a way back to his home and his dear Papa.

"Hey!" Lauren said suddenly. "Your Majesty! I think we can help you. Or rather, I think that you can help us. I think you have helped us, very much!"

The prince stopped pouting for a moment. "But I can't help you," he said. "I'm not on a quest. And I'm not going on a quest, if that's your idea."

"Oh, no, no," Lauren said. "Michael, please take out the Magic Book." So Michael opened the bag and took out the book, and handed it to Lauren. She invited the prince to come over. Her friends crowded around the Magic Book, too. The purple prince stared at the pictures. Then Lauren began to draw a new one. "Look what you've given us, your Majesty. This is a Magic Book of letters, and now I'm going to draw what's in front of me. Here's your purple palace, and here's the pillar popping purple popcorn, and here you are, pouting. And the pillar and the popcorn look sort of like the letter P. And so, in fact, do you! Do you see what you've given us?" And as she said that, there was a mighty POOF!

The pouting purple prince and the palace and the pillar and the popcorn all vanished in an instant. The four children found themselves alone on the beach. Lauren was standing up with the Magic Book open in her hands. "He really did help us. Poor prince," she said kindly. There were heavy clouds in the distance and it seemed as though it might rain.

"He's really okay now," Michael said. "He managed to get himself home."

"Which is more than we can do for ourselves," Rukmini said. "I wish we knew where we were, and I wish we could find our boat."

"Me too," Michael said. "But remember what the Hermit said."

The clouds, which had been banking on the horizon, moved closer and blocked the sun. A wind blew up, smelling of rain, and the sea grew dark.

All at once the children noticed how dark, how very dark, in fact, the sea had grown. In seconds, it had changed from a pale green to a much darker green. Then it went from dark green to a murky brown. And then it began to froth and foam and seethe as though something enormous was stirring it up. A giant swell grew not far from the shore, and the children turned to look at it.

seventeen

"QUICK!" yelled Michael. "Run for higher ground!" He took Rukmini by the hand, and she took Sipho by the hand, and he took Lauren by the hand, and they ran, carrying all they had, up and up and away from the beach. Sand and rocks tumbled beneath their feet as they scrambled up a rocky embankment. When they reached the top, they looked back and saw that the swollen sea had crashed onto the shore, swallowing up the whole beach and swirling onward and upward to the cliff where they stood.

It stopped just at the edge of the cliff. White foam licked the rocks they'd just climbed over. The children caught their breath. "Let's keep going," Sipho said. "We can't stop now. It feels like we're being chased. Once I was with my father in the bush and lions were stalking us. This is what it felt like. We got away because we were much cleverer than they were."

On they went, without looking back, their legs tired and aching, their arms scratched by trees and branches, until the wide silence and the distant rumble of the sea told them that they were far enough away to rest and take stock of their surroundings. Great drops of rain began to fall and the children saw that they were walking along a plain. There were a few sparse trees and hills with nowhere to take shelter from a storm. The sky was dark enough that the dormouse awoke and poked his head out of the bag.

"You missed all the excitement, dormouse!" Michael said.

"Oh, no, no, no, I didn't. I was simply hiding. But I was not asleep. Not a wink did I have, believe it or not. How could any living thing sleep through all that?" he said, scratching his whiskers to wake himself up. "Now listen, come closer, my voice is going all whispery and I can't make it go loud." The children all came closer and listened.

"Sipho's right," whispered the dormouse. "We are being chased. I didn't want to say it, I really didn't. He's after us and the Magic Book, because if he eats it we will lose all capacity for language. Do you see?" We will lose every letter that you found and every sound that each letter makes, and no one will be able to make any more words at all. And he will grow huge and eventually devour everything in this bright world."

"Who's chasing us, dormouse? Tell us!" Rukmini said urgently. It was beginning to pour now.

"Urckl, of course," Michael said, putting everything together in his mind.

"Shhh, not so loud," the dormouse said and put a paw to his mouth to hush them.

"Urckl, the sea monster—the huge shadow beneath the waves. Urckl is the chaser of the dolphin and the master of the dwarf of the door who had managed to steal all the D's. Does everyone see?" Michael continued. "Urckl wants the Magic Book!"

The children all nodded solemnly. They were soaking wet.

"What are we to do?" Rukmini asked finally.

"Look into the opal, Lauren, and tell us," the dormouse said.

"Oh, yes! My precious opal! I'd almost forgotten it," Lauren said. Excitedly she fumbled in her pocket and there, smooth and cool between her fingers, she found the beautiful stone. The children all crowded around to look at it. It was a beautiful deep blue color. They could see the heavy storm clouds in the stone, and the light changed as rain fell onto it. Lauren wiped away the rain with her hand, and as she did so, reflected in the stone, the children saw the dark clouds parting, and then shining stars peeping out and soft white clouds drifting across the sky.

"It's beautiful," Lauren breathed. As they stared, they all felt as though the vision they were seeing in the stone became enormous. Lauren felt herself beginning to spin and fall. She held onto Rukmini, who also felt as though she'd lost her balance. Then Michael and Sipho both grabbed tight hold of the dormouse. They all were truly spinning around, falling into the exquisite sky that waited to embrace them in the stone's reflection.

When the spinning stopped, the children were sitting right on top of the softest, fluffiest clouds, high in the night sky. The moon shone through the higher mountains of mist, and lit up millions of sparkling crystals embedded in the billowing clouds.

Rukmini found herself sitting in a cloud cave, on top of a dazzling crystal, and when she looked up, she saw, standing quietly above her, and looking very much like her aunt Chitra in India, a glorious queen holding an armful of crystals.

"Hello, Rukmini," said the Queen very quietly "I am the Quiet Queen of Dreams. I have come to help you and your friends."

"Thank you," Rukmini murmured, and glanced over her shoulder to see if her friends could see the queen too. She didn't know where they were, but it was so quiet, she hoped they were listening from their places in the clouds.

"No need for thanks. I must be quick. These crystals are for you and all your friends. As you take the crystals in your hands, they will seem to dissolve as you touch them, but truly, they will become a part of you, the part that is clear and full of courage. Whenever you are afraid, remember the clarity of crystals and you will quell fear in an instant. The journey ahead is quirky and full of quarrelsome and quaint creatures, some of them not so good, and some of them quite kind and helpful. Take heart, my dear, and take these, giving one to each of your friends." The Queen handed Rukmini five bright, sharp crystals. As she gratefully accepted them, she fell through the clouds and spun around until she landed softly on the ground next to Lauren and Michael and Sipho and the dormouse. Lauren held the cool opal in her hand. The storm had passed and a bright moon lit up the night.

"What are those?" the friends whispered in astonishment.

"Crystals for courage," Rukmini said, "from the Quiet Queen of dreams. One for you, Michael, one for you, Sipho, one for you, Lauren, and one for you, dear dormouse."

As each one took a crystal, it dissolved into shards of pure light. At that moment courage glowed within each one of the children, and they knew they could face their fear of the sea monster and continue their journey to take the Magic Book safely to the castle of the Wise Enchanter.

"Where is the Magic Book?" Rukmini asked softly. "I have to draw her quickly, and quietly. The Quiet Queen of Dreams gave us another letter."

"Yes," said her friends at once. "We saw her too."

"She was so beautiful," Sipho said. "We were further away than you were, but we still saw her. She gave us the crystals and the letter Q."

By the light of the moon, this is exactly what Rukmini drew.

eighteen

RESTLESS dreams finally woke Michael. He saw that they'd all fallen asleep next to the Magic Book, and Sipho was lying on it, holding it tightly. By the position of the moon in the sky and the darkness of the night, he guessed it was probably somewhere near midnight. There was so much light from the big moon that he could see everything as clearly as if it were day. In the distance he saw what he thought was a low, brick wall. This surprised him. The night felt heavy, as if the sky were pressing down on the earth. He looked around for the dormouse, but he was nowhere to be seen. Michael got up to see if he could find the dormouse. He wandered over the wide, sparse plain toward the low brick wall and a lonely tree whose branches caught the light of the setting moon.

Suddenly, the dormouse exploded out of a clump of grass and leapt right into Michael's arms, almost knocking him over. Before he could say anything, the dormouse put both paws on Michael's lips.

"Don't make a sound," he whispered. "One of his messengers is right here. And there are more, to be sure. They know about the Magic Book. Look what's happened!"

"What?" Michael had no idea where to look or what the dormouse was talking about.

"The brick walls!" the dormouse said. "They used to be part of a building, a respectable place of learning. Now it's all turning to dust. The walls have collapsed. No one learns anything anymore. The words to tell of its history are gone—have been gone for the longest time. Trust me, I've lived in the Enchanted Islands for more years than you or I could count. We need to find our way out of this place, but you must see what I mean first."

Michael and the dormouse crept quietly toward the ruins of the ancient place of learning. As they came closer, they heard strange noises: hinges opened and closed. Something banged. There was a rustling and then a muttering, or rather a loud grumbling. Michael held his breath.

Beyond the wall he could see a figure. It was clear that the fellow was some kind of a rogue, for he was shouting and mumbling to himself as he scrabbled around in a giant treasure chest, the lid of which was slightly open so that Michael and the dormouse could see that something within the chest glowed.

"Treasure!" Michael whispered. "He's some kind of pirate! What does he have in the chest?"

He managed to hold his voice down to a whisper, and the dormouse looked at him with solemn eyes. "The most precious treasure in the world," the dormouse hissed through his front teeth. Michael inched closer until he was standing right up against the old stone walls and could feel them cool beneath his palms. The rogue took some of the treasure and stuffed it into a huge bag, which he held in front of him. Then he took more and more. A peculiar whispering filled the air. The whispering sounded mournful and appeared to be coming straight from the treasure chest, and also from the sack. Michael noticed that the treasure seemed to be shimmering, moving, squirming, and jumping. "What IS it? What's he got there?"

"Words," said the dormouse softly, "thousands of bright words that haven't been used for a long time. They're so precious that no treasure in the world is more valuable. The robber takes the shining words and feeds them to Urckl, who eats them and grows stronger, and as the light of each word vanishes, the world grows darker. Now you have seen. Look. Do you see eyes in the darkness near the tree? Foxes. More messengers. I'll bet they're out snooping for more words. Maybe they have already caught wind of the Magic Book and are on their way to sniff it out. Wouldn't surprise me, no sirree. Listen, I've found a burrow nearby, which leads underground into a large cave. I think we might be safe there for a while. We need to wake the others and make haste."

"Wait, dormouse. Wait. The round bag that the robber's holding so roguishly—I see something there, in the way he's standing. He might be taking words, but he has no idea that I'm taking something from him. I have it! Quick, let's get to the Magic Book so that I can draw what I've seen. Then, I promise, we'll run far, far away from these rascals."

The dormouse sunk his claws into Michael's shoulder, scratching him as he held on for dear life, while Michael ran back to where the others were still fast asleep.

He found the Magic Book tucked away in a bag, though he remembered Sipho resting his head on it as he fell asleep. He didn't think to check on his friends right then, but he looked over his shoulder to be sure no one was following him. Quickly, he drew what he'd seen. The urgent scratching of his drawing on the paper woke Rukmini from her faraway dreams.

"What are you drawing?" she asked, half asleep.

"It's a raggedy rascally robber, robbing the world of words. Standing there with his round sack, he didn't know it, but he gave us the R!"

The page shone as if the picture were alive, and a shiver went down Michael's spine. "Where have you been?" Rukmini asked. And then she looked around her and cried out.

nineteen

"SIPHO! Where are you?" Her voice echoed across the wide empty landscape. Lauren opened her eyes and sat up. Michael shut the Magic Book, packed it deep into a bag, and looked from the dormouse to his friends.

"Where is he?" Michael burst out. "He was here just a few minutes ago. I'm sure he was...I...I saw him sleeping here...on the Magic Book, between you two!"

"Maybe he wandered off to find you!" Rukmini said to Michael.

"Oh oh oh," the dormouse cried and rubbed his head furiously in distress. "I'm supposed to be the night watchman! Oh, this will never do!"

"Okay," Michael said softly, "we have to be calm. He can't be too far away."

"But he can, he can," wailed the dormouse. "He could have been taken, by one of *them.* He could have...." The dormouse was so upset he choked on the rest of his words.

"I know we'll find him," Michael said. "Even if he's been taken—even he's very far away. Something happened while we weren't paying attention."

"I'm not going anywhere without him," Rukmini said.

Just then, the grass rustled and the moonlight caught yellow eyes that moved closer through the night. The dormouse leapt right up onto Rukmini's shirt.

"Urckl's foxes!" he shouted. "Run!"

"Run!" called Michael and grabbed the bag with the Magic Book and then Rukmini by the hand. Lauren followed quickly, pulling the rest of their belongings with them.

"Faster," urged the dormouse in Rukmini's ear. "We just have to get over the mound. On the other side is a burrow. Climb into it and move along the passageway. We can block the entrance easily." Rukmini ran with all the strength she had and came to the mound, went over it, and threw herself headlong into the burrow, tunneling her way deeper into the earth so that the others could follow. She heard Lauren and Michael come in.

"Stop the entrance. Use rocks, mud, anything," the dormouse wheezed.

As Michael was the nearest one to the entrance, he worked furiously with all he could find, until the entrance was completely blocked and the three children lay breathing hard in the darkness.

The foxes may have scratched and sniffed at the blocked burrow, but rocks and sticks and mud lay thick at the entrance, and the children heard nothing.

"If you'll all just move on ahead," said the dormouse. "You'll find we have much more room."

"What if Sipho's just out looking for Michael and he comes back and we're gone and the foxes..."

"Shhh," Michael whispered. "We'll find him." They crept deeper into the tunnel, which began to widen. It seemed to be much lighter at the end. When they got there, it opened out into a large underground cave. They could hear water dripping, and then they saw that the cave was open at the other end and right above them, and that the light they were seeing came from the early morning sky.

They walked through the cave and out into the dawn. A beautiful sight met their eyes: it was spring! There were flowers everywhere and birds sang. Butterflies kissed the flowers and an early morning breeze played music through the leaves of a large tree. The friends sat down on a circle of rocks and surveyed their surroundings.

"So, you've seen the spring," said a voice at Lauren's feet. She looked down and her eyes grew wide.

"Looked like snow yesterday, but you arrived and…well, spring's just spontaneously sprung out of the ground, so to say. Spontaneous spring's a bit suspect, if I say so myself, but so what! So…say something! Why so sullen? What's so special about a speaking snake! Yes I speak, of course I do. I'm so sick of silence…no one around here speaks anymore. …"

"I do," said the dormouse.

"Splendid!" said the snake, and flicked his small black tongue out to taste the air.

"We've lost our friend Sipho," Rukmini said. Have you seen him?"

"Sipho?" said the snake. "Sorry, it seems I haven't. Still, I'm sure he's somewhere. I'll slither along and you follow. Saying of the day is: searchers, seeking Sipho. He should be somewhere."

"It's really quite serious," Rukmini said.

"Certainly, certainly," said the snake. "If I can be of service, I shall. Follow me."

The speaking serpent slithered through the spring grass, and the three children followed. After several hours they sat down to rest and the snake stood up on his tail and cast a beady eye over the surrounding fields.

"Sipho, you say," he said thoughtfully. "About your age?"

"Yes!" said Rukmini. "We're afraid he's been stolen."

Lauren looked at the snake as he spoke. Then she bent her head to whisper in Rukmini's ear. "See the shape of the speaking snake? He's an exact S."

"Sketch him while you can," Rukmini replied. Her heart grew lighter. If—even as they searched for Sipho—they were still discovering letters, then surely they were not going the wrong way entirely.

"Dear snake, may I sketch you? You have such a perfect shape!"

"Certainly," said the snake, and blinked. He was flattered. "Make sure you get my scales, see?"

"Yes," smiled Lauren, and she drew the swirling S shape of the speaking serpent.

As she finished, Rukmini suddenly looked at her. "Oh, Lauren," she exclaimed. "I had completely forgotten! Use the opal. It might show us exactly where Sipho is!"

"Of course!" said Lauren, and found the stone. She held it in front of her. At first the stone only reflected the blue sky, but then a strange mist shifted across the surface. When it cleared, Rukmini shouted for joy.

"I see him! I see him!"

"So long then," said the snake. "I'll just sit and savor the spontaneous spring. It should disappear shortly. Suppose I'll be seeing you sometime." He was about to slither off when Lauren turned to him.

"Thank you, snake," she said, "for showing us the way here. We might otherwise never have thought of the opal. And thank you especially for your shape."

"Salutations then," he said and bowed his head. Then he slithered off into the soft spring grass.

twenty

THAT night Sipho had been awakened by something trying to nudge the Magic Book out from under him. When he opened his eyes a cloud had crossed in front of the moon and it was so dark that he could see nothing. Then he'd felt something nudging him, trying to push him aside. Without thinking any further, he knew what he had to do. He grabbed hold of the Magic Book for dear life. Then he got up on his knees and crawled, elbows first, toward the bag that usually kept the Magic Book. Whatever was nosing around backed off for an instant. The book seemed to weigh a ton in his hands, and he fumbled for the bag and then dropped the book in the shadows next to his sleeping friends and ran into the night.

Something chased him. He knew it was an animal, but it ran lightly and soundlessly across the ground and seemed to always be the exact same distance behind him. Just as Sipho was tiring, the moon came out from behind the cloud and he saw, too late, a hole in the ground in front of him. He tumbled into it.

He fell a long way, but hit the ground without hurting himself. When he looked around, he saw that he was inside a cave. The entrance was just an arm's length away and whatever had been chasing him was no longer to be heard and hadn't fallen with him into the hole.

Sipho crept carefully outside. He could smell that the dawn was not far off. The night stars were dipping below the horizon and he could smell the sweet fragrance of spring in the air. He looked behind him. There was nothing there. The landscape, he could tell, was no longer so sparse. In the distance he could hear the rumbling of water and he knew he'd left whatever was chasing him in another place altogether.

Fearing that the Magic Book would be gone, but trusting that his friends would use their gifts to find him, Sipho began to walk wearily toward the sound of the water.

As the sun slowly rose, light caught swirls of mist rising up from the dense, grassy bush ahead. Flowers opened and sweet smells filled the air. Birds sang songs he thought he remembered from Africa. Grass grew knee high, and there, beyond the tall canopy of a tree, was a thundering waterfall that plunged deep into a distant valley.

Sipho lay down under the tree at the edge of the waterfall. As the sun burned off the night's chill, he fell into an exhausted sleep.

"I see him, I see him!"

At first he was certain the voices were part of a dream. But as they became more insistent, he realized that they came from outside the realm of dreams.

"There he is! Oh, it's just like it looked in the magic opal. There's the opening to the cave, there's the tree and there's the huge waterfall."

"Sipho! Are you all right? Please tell us you're okay!"

He opened his eyes and the sunlight almost blinded him. Three faces peered down at him anxiously. Then the dormouse jumped down out of a bag and ran all over him, sniffing him and making sure that he was intact and that no harm had come to him.

"I'm really okay," Sipho said. "Do you have the Magic Book?"

"Safe and sound," Lauren said. "We thought Urckl's messengers had taken you away."

"I was chased by wolves, or foxes, or perhaps some kind of wild dogs. But they couldn't catch me. They don't know I've been running away from animals all my life. I think they thought I had the Magic Book with me."

The children laughed and sat down in the grass next to Sipho, and hugged him.

"Those were Urckl's foxes," Michael said. "And I'm certain they wanted the Magic Book. Their eyesight can't be very good! The book was just lying there beneath the stars."

"It feels better here," Lauren said, "as if the heaviness of the wide open plains has been left behind for a while."

"I think they've lost our scent," Michael said. "We should be able to travel for a bit without being followed."

"I hope so," said Rukmini.

"Let's get out the Magic Book and show Sipho the Speaking Snake," Lauren said. As soon as the book was out of the bag, the dormouse crept into the space and made himself comfortable in a corner of the bag. Lauren opened the book and they all looked at the beautiful S shape of the Speaking Snake. Sipho got up after a minute and looked at the waterfall.

"I'm just going to see if there's any way we can follow the river before anything follows us. All waterways must eventually lead to the sea, and this time we might find a coastline that we recognize." He walked toward the edge of the waterfall and looked down into the foaming currents below. As he stood there beneath the tree, Lauren, with her keen eyes and the Magic Book open before her, tapped Michael on the shoulder and pointed.

"What is it?" Michael asked.

"Sipho!" Lauren called, beckoning to him. He came running back.

"Look at the tree," she said.

"It's an umbrella tree! I know these trees. In Africa they are the helpers. Their wide branches protect you from the sun, and their dark shadows hide you from anything that's chasing you. And I do see something," Sipho nodded. "The tree with its wide, shady branches is a T. The symbol that comes after S is T. I thought we were losing our way. May I draw it?"

"Yes," Lauren said, handing him the book. "And draw yourself underneath it." So Sipho did. He drew a strong, sturdy tree, whose arms reached out over the land and gave shelter to all who needed it. And there it was, the letter T. The image shone as if the heat of an African day suffused the page. Everyone took a deep breath.

Then they wrapped the book in several layers of clothes and packed it into another bag, so as not to disturb the sleeping dormouse.

twenty-one

UNDER the shade of the umbrella tree, after a meal in which everyone ate as if they hadn't eaten for days, the children packed up what remained of their things. Clouds formed in the distance as the children started on their journey down stream. The path was narrow and the rushing waters below churned and frothed as they tumbled over rocks and boulders.

"All rivers lead to the sea," Michael repeated. "Maybe this time we'll find our boat."

They walked for many hours. The wind grew colder and blew racing clouds across the sky and across the sun. The pathway narrowed.

"It's cooling down again," Lauren said. They stopped for a minute to take out some warm clothes.

"There's a dip on this side of the pathway," Michael said. "I'm just going to see what's down there. Maybe there's a better place to walk."

He took a few steps through the grass and underbrush. Then he lost his footing and tumbled head over heals through greenery. A rushing whispering sound filled his ears and he fancied that he had been stolen, too, by some of Urckl's messengers.

"Help!" he called out, pulling leaves out of his hair as he came to rest at the bottom of a big ditch. The whispering in his ears grew louder and he looked around for his friends. Surely they must have heard him calling! He expected that at any moment Urckl's foxes would spring out of the enormous leaves. He closed his eyes tightly, waiting to be found.

"He's not very ugly, is he?" said a voice.

"No, his face is kind."

"Is he dead?"

"No, no. Maybe he's sleeping."

"I haven't seen one of these for ever so long. What is it?"

"A child. A real human child."

Something tickled Michael's arm and he dared to open one eye. Then he opened both eyes in astonishment. Sitting in the crook of his arm was the tiniest, palest, most delicate little person he'd ever seen. Her skin was so pale Michael could almost see through it. Her eyes were dark and solemn.

"He's not dead, not sleeping either," said the little thing. "What's your name child?"

Michael looked around. On every side, under every leaf and stalk, he saw them now. There were hundreds of them. They were all dressed in greens and grays and dark blues. All of them looked at him out of dark eyes. Their pale little faces creased with curiosity as Michael struggled to sit up.

"I'm...Michael. What are you?"

"We," said the little person on his arm, "are Underlings."

"Weren't always," piped another from his place under a leaf.

"Won't always be," chirped another from under a stalk.

"Shhh. We don't know that," said the one on Michael's arm.

"What's that?" Michael enquired, sitting up now. "What is an Underling?"

"We live underneath everything," said Michael's Underling.

"We had to go under—under bushes, under trees, under leaves. Under, under, under—we never go up. Can't go up. It's become too cold. It used to be cool, but now it stays cold. And there are too many big, insensitive walkers with heavy feet stomping around on top, so it's too dangerous for us. We're on an underneath journey to recover something we've lost, but now we are lost too. So here we sit, under the leaves, uninspired to continue."

"Michael! Are you okay?" Rukmini's head peered down from the top of the ditch.

"I'm not hurt at all," he replied. "Come down here. Tell the others to come too, but be careful; don't touch any of the leaves."

"Okay," Rukmini called. "We're coming." Her head vanished again, and Michael looked at the Underling on his arm.

"I have three friends and a dormouse," he said. "None of us will do you any harm."

The others came down into the dip carefully.

"What is it?" Lauren asked as Michael put his fingers to his lips. Then he pointed to the green leaves. His three friends, carrying only the Magic Book and the dormouse, came creeping up to him. Their eyes followed the direction of his fingers, and then Lauren looked at his arm and gave a little squeal of delight.

"Fairies!" she exclaimed breathlessly. "Oh, how very beautiful."

The Underling on Michael's arm very sadly and slowly shook her head.

"Not fairies," Michael said. "Underlings. They have no wings." All the tiny faces in the bushes grew immediately sorrowful.

The children could not believe their eyes. They looked at all the pale little faces peering out at them from the undergrowth, and for a while no one had anything to say. Then Michael said, "We're on a journey too. We're trying to find the castle of the Wise Enchanter. And now the monster Urckl and his messengers are afoot, and we have to beware of them."

There was immediately such excited chatter among the little folk that it seemed to the four children as though a strong gust of wind had blown through the ditch, rustling all the leaves against one another. The Underlings came creeping out into the light, closer to the children, shielding their eyes against the brightness of the day.

"Take us with you," said an Underling who looked like he might be some sort of leader. "We will be your travel guides if you will carry us with you."

The children looked at the hundreds of little faces. "How can we carry you?" Rukmini asked.

"There are two hundred of us. We'll fit anywhere," said the leader, looking up at the big children who stood over them. "Bags, pockets, shoulders, anywhere—you don't have to worry about us. Try it! It's easy. Yes! We are coming with you to the castle of the Wise Enchanter!" The leader grabbed onto Michael's leg as though he did not plan to let it go, ever.

Michael and his friends exchanged glances. Then they nodded kindly at the Underlings who ran out from under the underbrush with whoops of delight, and began climbing up the children's legs, onto their backs, into their pockets, onto their heads, and into the bags they carried. Michael sat down to allow them to climb up onto him more easily.

Then the children made ready to climb up out of the undergrowth. In their pockets and their bags and holding onto their arms and in the creases and folds of their clothes, the four children carried two hundred and one Underlings (for they had miscounted by one).

Up and up they climbed to find the path again that they would all follow down stream.

As he looked along the great, wide ditch ahead of them, Michael whispered to Lauren. "Let me have the Magic Book."

When he had the book, he began to draw. Two curious Underlings perched on his shoulder. "What Is it?" "What are you drawing?"

"Here it is. Thank you, Underlings," Michael said. "Look, everyone! The underbrush in the dip has made the letter U. The Underlings have given us the sound of their name, and the undergrowth has given us the shape of the letter. We must surely find the Wise Enchanter before it is too late."

Just as he said that, a freezing wind whipped through their hair.

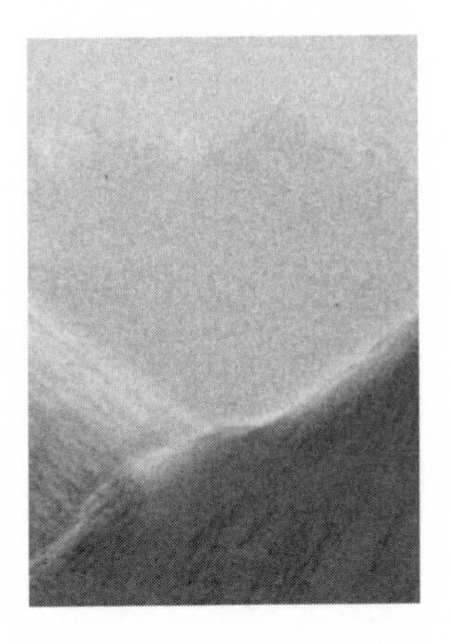

twenty-two

VERY carefully, they picked their way along the pathway, choosing each step with caution. Soon it seemed that they were walking along nothing more than a rocky ledge that fell away into the steep gorge made by the river. The chill air around them became heavy. They had to push against it in order to move forward, and the distance between the ledge and the swirling waters seemed greater and greater by the moment. The grass rustled; a strange wind blew. Rukmini stopped, her ears tuned to the sounds. They all waited and watched.

"What is it?" Lauren whispered.

"I don't know," Rukmini replied. "I feel something. We must hurry up." They began to walk again.

Afternoon wore on, and the sun came out from behind clouds but did little to warm the children. The Underlings, tucked safely away, were protected from the cold, as was the dormouse, who was fast asleep and knew nothing of the cold or the Underlings. At last, the rocky ledge came to an end and they found themselves walking on rich, green grass. They could still hear the river and continued on, following its sound. As they looked at the grass they noticed how the edges were turning brown, as if each blade had been touched by a frost overnight and was losing its life and color.

* * *

Far away, through the clouds and mists and over many waves of blue and green and silver, in a room at the top of the castle with spires that reached up into the heavens, Gadrun knelt at her father's bedside. It was late afternoon and already dark as if it were night. Icicles clung to the castle walls and hung down from the tall spires.

Tears rolled down Gadrun's beautiful cheeks as she took her father's hand. "It won't be long now, dear father. They will be here. I can feel them getting nearer. Surely you know that."

"Ah yes, my child. But they may be too late. For me, they may be too late. The light has become so weak that I can scarcely move my head. Words have been vanishing from the world so quickly, and with them go all thoughts, all Wisdom. I fear it is the loss that weakens me. The darkness grows stronger. Urckl's appetite is immense. He is rising from the deep, and soon he will devour everything, and even I will be too weak to resist him, too weak to make my journey to the Everlasting Islands."

Gadrun looked at her father. "Father, I will not let that happen. The children will arrive here safely with their Magic Book in which they are carefully keeping every symbol that they find. When you have this before your eyes, your strength will return."

"Tell me," he said softly. "Do you believe that after all their adventures they are still unselfish and kind?"

"I believe they are."

"If they are not, they will never be able to conquer what lies ahead of them."

"I believe that their hearts are true, and that no selfish thoughts have entered their minds, nor unkind words come from their lips."

Gadrun pressed her father's cool hand between her two warm ones. He looked at her and tried to smile. Then he sighed and let his head fall back against the soft pillow.

The waves crashed over Gadrun's feet. She called over the wind, uttering a strange sound that traveled over and under the water, far and fast as any echo. After a while, bubbles rose in the water in front of her, and the sea sprite emerged sparkling from the deep.

"You called, your Majesty?"

"Thank you for coming. I may not travel as a dolphin, and yet I fear greatly for our four young friends. Look, the clouds are dark; the cold has set in. People's thoughts are murky and grim. Now Urckl knows that the children have many stories, and I fear that he will try to do great harm. This cannot happen. Is there anything you can do?"

"I will keep watch over them, your Majesty. They have gone far from the sea and lost their boat and I've been waiting for them to return to the water. While I cannot fight off a beast such as Urckl, I can guide our friends, unseen. I can do a few things to make it easier for them and warn them if danger approaches."

"Thank you," Gadrun said. "That's all I ask." Her lovely face was as pale as the ice that clung to the castle. The sea sprite bowed her head and then splashed back into the water and swam swiftly away.

* * *

"We're starting to go downhill, I can feel it."

"It's definitely steeper."

"And colder."

"Look, the river's getting narrower! There's a valley below!"

"Lots of valleys!"

The children talked rapidly. They were cold now, and the sun did little to warm them. The Underling who had been on Michael's arm now rode along on his shoulder and whispered in his ear.

"I do know this place," she said. "This must be the Land of a Thousand Valleys. We used to come here when... when...." She stopped talking. Michael couldn't see why she was suddenly quiet, but then he thought he heard her choking, or coughing, or sobbing.

"Does anyone know if this leads to the sea?" Michael asked.

"The sea, the sea!" chanted the Underling on his shoulder.

The path led them down and down and down. Down they went from one level to the next. Each time they descended, the river became smaller. Less water cascaded down over rocks.

"Maybe the river goes underground," Sipho said, "and then we won't know if it goes to the sea." But hardly had the words escaped his lips, when a gust of salty, cold air blew into their faces.

The children stopped where they were. They turned to look back on the way that they'd come. Sipho was tired and sat down at the edge of the river. He had been carrying the Magic Book, which seemed to be suddenly filled with lead. He felt he'd just had the weight of the world on his shoulders and he let the bag with the Magic Book fall to the ground.

As he gazed at the valleys through which they had come, the sun appeared from the clouds to shine on the sharp inclines. The light illuminated a valley's shape, and at the same time the other children saw what Sipho did.

"There's a letter in the land," he said. "The valley is a V!" He was almost too weak to lift the Magic Book. Rukmini rushed over to help him lift it onto his lap. They all looked at the big, deep V of the valley through which they had just descended. The sides were steep, and it seemed impossible that they had come all the way down there without falling hundreds of feet down into the river. The moment Sipho's drawing was complete, the sun vanished again, but the page shone for a few moments after the light had gone. Sipho closed the Magic Book. The dormouse stirred in his bag and tried to make himself more comfortable. Then he suddenly poked his head through the opening.

"What is it?" he asked, sniffing the air.

"The letter V," Sipho replied.

"No, no! What's the smell?"

"Oh, you've smelled them at last. The Underlings." Lauren said. "Allow me to introduce you."

Some little pale faces appeared, rather cautiously, from everywhere, and looked curiously at the perplexed dormouse.

"Nope," he said slowly, eyeing the underlings. "That's not what I smell."

twenty-three

"WHAT is it, then?" Lauren asked, and they all turned to look ahead of them.

"The sea!" Rukmini called out at the top of her lungs. "I see the sea!" Evening was beginning to descend and the smell of the briny air brought memories of sailing to the children's minds. But now they could not make themselves warm. The air coming off the water bit into their cheeks and made them numb.

The sky grew dark so that soon the only things the children could see were the white froth on the wave's edges and a sad, full moon that peeped hesitantly now and then from behind the racing, grim clouds. Rukmini was uneasy. All the Underlings had hidden themselves so well now that none were to be seen. The children were weary; the only person wide awake was the dormouse, full of the energy of a brand new day and ready to organize everybody.

"No time to waste," he said efficiently. "We must get down to the beach. If we find our boat, we must set sail tonight. With or without the sea monster, the only way to the castle of the Wise Enchanter is across the water. Time is running out. We must go."

"Yes, dear dormouse," sighed Lauren. "But have a heart. We've just had a full day of adventuring and need a moment to gather our strength."

"Yes, yes, I see," said the dormouse, not seeing. "It's getting late, though. We must hurry."

The children climbed down grassy, sandy banks until they stood on a beach that reminded them of something.

"I know!" Lauren said eagerly. "This looks like the place where we left the prince of the purple palace. Only," she added, "there's no trace of our having been here." She paused. "Maybe it isn't the same spot after all," she concluded glumly.

Far down the beach and heading toward the shore, a little boat bobbed about on the dark waters. It was wandering in a certain direction, and it certainly wasn't alone. Beneath the green waves lived many beings, and some of them were kind and good. Gentle hands now tugged and pushed and guided until the vessel, once floating aimlessly and empty in the waves that had almost swallowed it, ran aground. The bottom scraped roughly against the sand in the moonlight. The noise startled the four children waiting on the beach.

"What's that?" Rukmini gasped.

"Something's there! Look," Sipho whispered.

For a while no one was sure whether to go toward the oblong shadow on the beach or run quickly away from it.

When they saw that it didn't move, and when they noticed by its shape that it had neither legs nor a head, they stepped gingerly toward it.

"I do declare," the dormouse announced, "that our long-lost boat has at last been found!"

"It *is* the boat," Michael called, and tired though he was, he leapt across the sand until he reached it. He grabbed the boat with both hands and hugged it as though it were some dear, old friend.

With cries of delight, Lauren and Rukmini danced over to the boat, and then around it, inspecting it, touching it, running their hands over the wood.

"It's in good shape," Michael announced.

"Sail's a bit tatty," Rukmini said. "But we can fix that."

"I stitch," said the Underling on Michael's shoulder, loud enough that everyone could hear. "If you have a needle and thread, I can do it."

Yes, the children did have a needle and thread, and even though night had fallen and the wind blew, and the sea was restless, the children worked industriously and courageously to get their boat fixed and fit for travel. The Underlings helped. One could stitch rapidly with a needle as big as she was. The other could seal small cracks and holes that no one else could see. And the dormouse watched and repeatedly urged everyone to hurry.

The wind blew harder. "Hurry up, hurry up," the dormouse chanted nervously. "We don't want anything to catch up with us. Let's go!"

Waves crashed along the shore, grinding the sand finer and drowning out all the children's voices.

"I don't think we should set sail now!" Rukmini shouted into the wind. "It's too wild!"

The wind whipped the sea into a frenzy. Waves thundered down.

"The boat won't make it in this weather!"

It was wintry and wet. From time to time rain fell from the sky.

Then, all at once the wind wiped the clouds from the moon. A wild wave welled up from the deep, washed by silvery moonlight. Lauren watched the wave, willing it to break far from them, wishing that it wouldn't be anything like the wave that had first sent them rushing fearfully away from the beach. Then an amazing thing happened. As she stood there, stunned by what she saw, the wave itself became a form. It was a sign, a symbol to be read, for those who had eyes to see, and only Lauren saw it.

"The wild wave is a W," she whispered to herself. "It must mean we can sail. No matter how dangerous it might seem, we're still finding the symbols we need."

"Wait!" she shouted to her friends who were busily tying up the sail and pulling the boat away from the sea. "Wait!" she called with all her might above the wind, as the wave finally broke and came crashing down on the shore. "We can brave these waves!"

Lauren took the heavy Magic Book onto her lap. With Michael standing over it and protecting it from the now-and-again night rain, Lauren drew a big, wild wavy W. The page looked wet and bright, though it remained, in fact, quite dry.

And then, heartened by the discovery of another precious symbol, the children decided that they would, indeed, brave the wild waters of the night. The dormouse gave instructions, the Underlings hid, and the children began to push the boat toward the thundering surf.

"Ubusika bufikile!" shouted Sipho, as his feet touched the water.

"What does that mean?" Rukmini shouted back.

"Winter is here," Sipho yelled.

"What language is that?" Rukmini called out loudly. She closed her eyes against the cold, wet wind and jumped into the boat as it made it over the first wave.

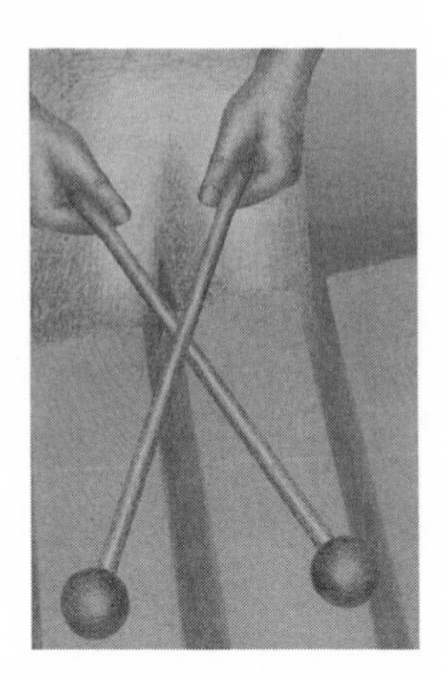

twenty-four

"XHOSA," Sipho called back, "the language of my grandmother on my father's side. *Nkosi, Ngiyabonga*. Thanks, in Xhosa and in Zulu, the languages of my father and my mother," he added, as Rukmini gave him a hand onto the boat. Then Sipho helped Michael and Lauren into the boat too.

"Aapka swagat hai," Rukmini said, turning her face away from the wind. "That means you're welcome in Hindi, the language of my grandmother. I don't remember it much anymore," she shouted. "But my grandmother doesn't want me to forget. So I will try not to...."

A big wave rocked the boat violently and the four children gripped the sides with all their might. The wind caught the sails, and suddenly the boat leapt across the waves, skimming readily over the choppy seas as if blown by some generous, knowing wind.

Against the cold wall of winter air, the boat sailed on. The children huddled down, rocked furiously from side to side. The sails bulged, filled with an icy wind that blew them onward into the open sea. The water was as dark as the night around them, but the dormouse's eyes gleamed, for he was awake and alert. Soon the wild waves calmed somewhat, and the four children fell into an uncomfortable but exhausted sleep.

The sky barely grew light when the sun came up. It was a small sun, a faraway sun in an expanse of misty, gray nothingness. The children slowly awoke and stretched their aching limbs. They were sailing between rocky islands, which stood starkly against the sky. None offered any place to land, so steep and craggy were their sides. The sea crashed around the rocks at the base of the cliffs. The children noticed that there were caves and holes in the rocks, as though the pounding waters had worn them down for centuries.

As they sailed very close to one of the big rocky outcrops, something bumped the bottom of the boat.

"What's that?" Rukmini said, hardly daring to breathe.

"It could be..." Lauren began.

"It's ice," Michael said. "Look around." Beneath them, around them, when they looked carefully, they could see that the water had formed into solid blue-gray lumps. The boat had wedged itself between rocks and ice. They looked up. "It's going to take a bit of work to free ourselves," Michael said.

"The rock is hollow up there. It looks like some kind of a cave entrance!" Sipho said.

"We could go in there and make a fire. I'm frozen," Lauren said. "I used to enjoy the cold and snow when we lived in Scotland, in the far north, but this is too cold even for me. I don't think I can manage to do anything until I'm warmer."

"Me too!"

"Me too."

"Let's take what we need and go up there."

With a strong piece of rope, they helped one another across the rocks and ice and up to the cave opening, taking only the Magic Book and whatever they needed for a fire.

As they climbed through the opening, Sipho ran his hands over the rocks. "This isn't just a cave," he said. "Someone has made this entrance. The rocks have been placed like this on purpose!"

"Yes," said Rukmini and crawled in after him. To her surprise, the the cave was light and bright, and reminded her of the inside of a beautiful shell. But that was not the end of the surprise. As they all stood together inside, the cave became more like a room than a cave, and they no longer noticed the cold at all. At the other end was an open door and through it they could see daylight—bright, beautiful sunshine, of the kind they hadn't seen for a very long time indeed. There was even grass and hills. Finally, they all noticed that there was something else in the room. It looked like a table. And behind that, to their amazement, someone sat.

The children had forgotten all about being cold. In fact, they were so warm that some of them began to peel off layers of clothing. They set down all their supplies for making a fire, and with that, all thoughts of making one. The person who sat at the other end of the room was a woman. She wore a blue cloak with a hood and she was bent over almost double with age. As they came closer to her, her midnight blue eyes rested on them. She lifted an ancient wrinkled face to greet them.

"What brings four children to the very end of the world?" she croaked.

"We're on a journey to find the castle of the Wise Enchanter," Sipho said, noticing at that moment that the table wasn't a table, but a beautiful musical instrument.

"He's ill," the old woman said gruffly.

"Ill?" said all four children at once. "How can that be?"

"It can be, in the same way that I am here, banished to reside in this cavern at the end of the world, when I used to be everywhere and anywhere. I fear you may be too late!"

"What?" Rukmini gasped. "We can't be too late, we can't!"

"Who are you, ma'am?" asked Michael politely, remembering what his grandparents had often told him about how to speak to older people.

"Madame Conch Ends," the children heard her say, and she smiled. "Mostly people know me only as a little voice telling them to apologize when they do something unkind, or reminding them to be unselfish and to consider others. But for a long time now, I've been ignored. For many years no one has heard me. I'm thus banished to the end of the world where I am of no use to anyone anymore."

"That's terrible," Rukmini said. "Can we do something to help you?"

"Good question, dearie," Madame Conch Ends said. Rukmini thought she saw tears glisten in the old lady's eyes. "I'm not sure you can, though. You can try. If you do succeed in your quest, you can know that I will immediately be set free, and will begin to expand over all the earth again so that everyone can hear my whispers. If you don't succeed, well, eventually the ice will enter here too, and I will freeze over. But, there is something I would very much enjoy right now. This instrument has been silent for as long as I have. Can any of you play it?"

"What is it?" Michael asked.

"A xylophone!" Lauren said. "A big, double one."

"It looks like something I played at school in Africa," Sipho said. "I know how to play the Marimba, so maybe I can play this."

"Go ahead, my boy," said Madame Conch Ends, and handed him two long poles with rubber ends.

The xylophone was a beautiful instrument, fashioned out of metal and wood. The metal pieces gleamed in the light that shone so unusually through the door at the end of the cavernous room—even though the vision of grass and hills and sunlight had now vanished. Each metal piece took on a color of the rainbow and, as Sipho began to play, the most beautiful music filled the room. Every note sounded like an enormous raindrop, round and pure and clear. As Sipho played one note after the other, they ran into each other, and Rukmini and Michael and Lauren and Madame Conch Ends and all the hidden Underlings felt like the music carried them far, far away from where they were.

"That is the music that could melt the heart of a monster," Madame Conch Ends said softly.

"Thank you!" Sipho said and smiled. "I...," he began and then stopped. He stared down at the sticks in his hands.

"What's the matter, boy?" Madame Conch Ends said.

"I'm making an X with the sticks in my hands!" he exclaimed. The other children bent over to look. "Yes! You are making an X over a xylophone. It's extraordinary!"

"We have the letter X! Thank you, Madame Conch Ends, thank you!" Sipho said.

"Excellent. May I give to you, the gift of the xylophone? It might be put to good use one day," she said.

"I'm afraid, though, that it's too big to carry with us in our little boat." Sipho said.

"You can make it small," Madame Conch Ends said and shrugged. "Just take it in your hand and press it."

Sipho looked at her and at his friends, bewildered. "Take it and press it small...?" he murmured. Then he went to the xylophone, took it gently by its edges, and in no time at all he held it in miniature in his hand.

"Now put it in your pocket," Madame Conch Ends said. "When you need it again, simply take it out and play!"

"Madame Conch Ends," Michael said, "I do hope that we won't be too late to rescue you. I would like to ask you so many things, like, why are you called Madame Conch Ends? Does that have anything to do with conch shells? Are they ending, the shells in the sea? Do you end them? Can they end you? But the inside of this cave looks like a giant conch shell, so I can't imagine that they are a danger to you."

She smiled at him. "You will understand one day, dear boy. Look."

He turned to see Lauren struggling to lift the Magic Book out of its bag. It took two children to lift it now. Sipho drew his hands making an X over the xylophone into the book, and then he put the little instrument carefully in a pocket that had buttons on it. "Thank you, again, Madame Conch Ends," he said and bowed to her, touching his hands together. "Especially for the warmth...it is so lovely and warm in here, and everywhere else is not."

Madame Conch Ends winked.

"Well, are we warm enough to be on our way?" he asked, turning to his friends.

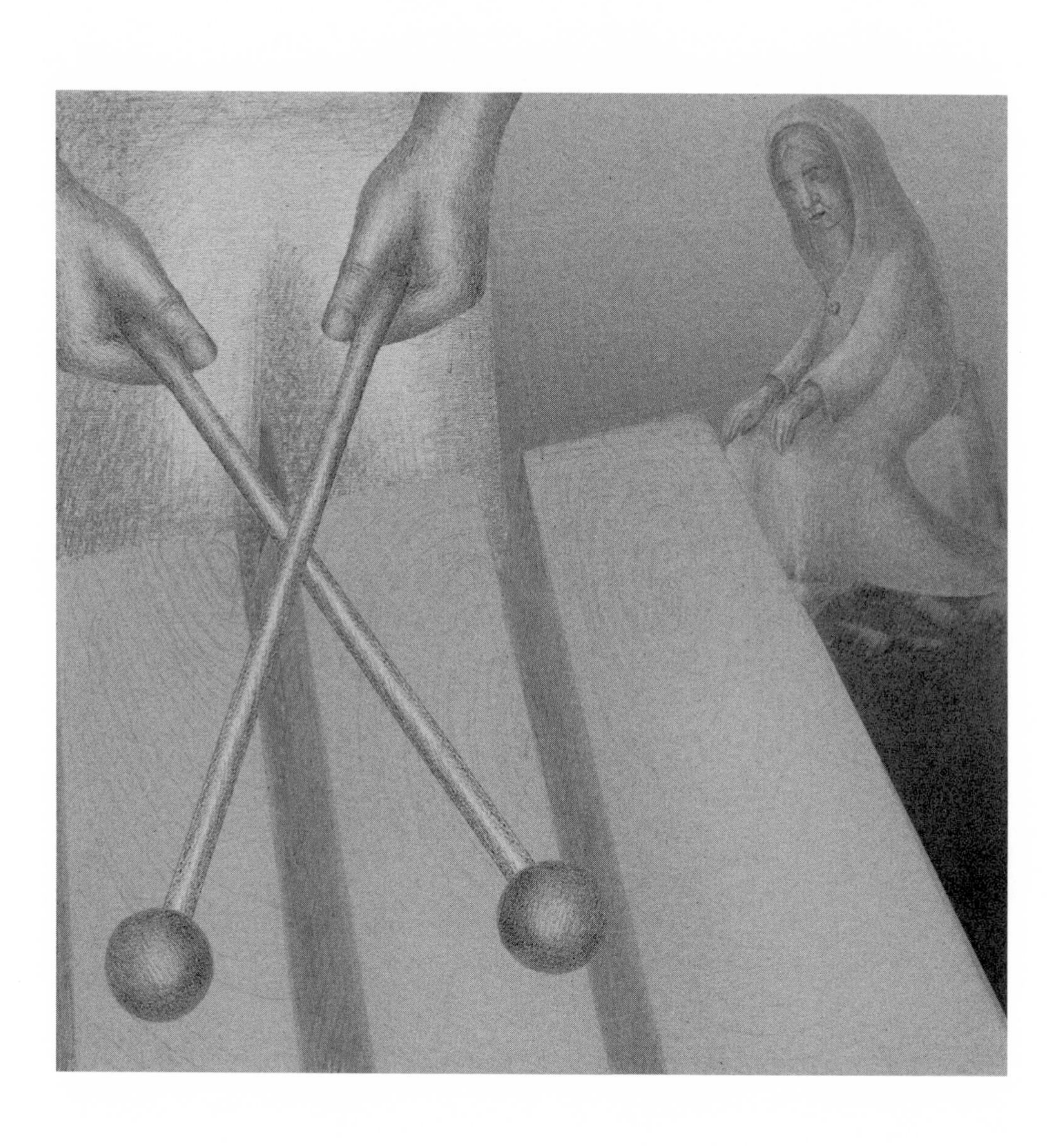

twenty-five

"YES," they all said, and took their leave of the kind old woman in the blue cloak.

When they crept outside again, the cold seemed more vicious than ever. Climbing back down to their boat, they noticed at once that the sea had frozen solid and that they could walk on it as though it were land.

"Oh, no," said Michael. "We can't sail on this!"

Using the rope and all their will power to get it out, the children managed to pull the boat free of the ice and onto the frozen sea. With the four of them tugging on the rope, heads bowed into the bitter weather, they began to walk and pull. The boat glided like a giant sled behind them. They stopped only once, and briefly, to eat something small. Then they continued, on and on.

"I'm tired," said Lauren.

Beneath their feet, the sea looked more and more like a frozen snowy land. They could still see the rocky islands, but soon even those were swallowed in fog, and before them stretched an endless, unbroken expanse of white.

Snow began to fall from the sky, and it was harder and harder to move.

"I don't think we can do this anymore," Rukmini whispered. "We're too late. The sun has vanished entirely."

Just then, there was a loud growl from the silent fog. Or perhaps it was a roar. Or maybe it was a rumble. The children cried out. Something heavy was moving toward them. The ice below their feet shook, and even the dormouse peeped out of his bag and sniffed the wind.

Something heavy thudded through the snow. Ahead of them, the children could see a great dark form. It thudded closer and closer.

All at once, an immense, hairy beast appeared in front of them. It had long, shaggy brown fur and big, wide horns and it snorted great puffs of white air.

"It's a…a…buffalo?" said Lauren weakly.

"A yak!" Michael said. "I've seen one before in a zoo."

"A yak?" Lauren exclaimed, as the creature snorted and looked at them intently. Then a deep voice rumbled toward them.

"Yes, yes! A yak."

"A talking yak? Did you say that, yak?" Michael asked.

"Why, yes," said the yak, and slowly, like a reluctant horse, ambled to where they stood.

"Oh, dear yak," Lauren pleaded. "We appear to have lost our way. Can you help us?"

"Yes, yes," said the yak, and nodded his head.

"Do you…happen to know the way to the castle of the Wise Enchanter?" Rukmini asked.

"Yes," said the yak.

"Are we going in the right direction?" Michael asked.

"Yes," said the yak.

The children smiled at one another. Through their smiles, their cheeks ached with cold.

"Is the castle very far away?" Sipho asked.

"Ye...es," said the yak.

"Can you say anything else besides yes?" asked Michael anxiously.

"Why, yes," said the yak. Michael threw up his hands.

"It's no use!" he cried out. "He says yes to everything! He can only say three words, why, yes, and yak! We might be a million miles away from the Wise Enchanter!"

An idea had just come to Lauren and she walked up to the yak and touched his soft brown nose. "Are you enchanted, yak?"

"Yes!" he snorted and stamped his feet and pawed the ground until ice flew.

"Oh, you poor, poor creature, whatever you are!" Lauren said and rubbed her hands together to make them warm. "Listen to me. If I ask you a question, and the answer is no, don't answer me, okay?"

"Yes," said the yak.

"Do you know the way to the castle of the Wise Enchanter?"

"Yes," said the yak.

"This might not work," Michael said. "He says yes to anything and everything."

"Do you say yes to anything and everything, yak?" Lauren asked.

The yak snorted and said nothing.

"Yay! That was a no!" Lauren cried out. "He does understand us! He can help us! Yak, may I travel on your back and place my hands in your warm, soft fur?"

"Yes, yes!" said the yak.

"Can we trust you?" asked Rukmini.

"Why, yes, YES!"

Lauren climbed up onto the warm back of the big, shaggy beast. There was so much room on his back that eventually Rukmini climbed up too. The yak's fur was as warm as a summer's day, and soon all four children and the dormouse were riding on the yak, while he pulled the boat effortlessly behind him through the ice and snow.

The children were so used to carrying the Underlings that they had almost forgotten about them, until one climbed up onto Lauren's shoulder and whispered in her ear, "I'm so very, very itchy!"

"You're probably too hot!" Lauren said. "Poor thing. Come out into the fresh air." So he did, for a while. Then another Underling appeared, reaching around and trying to scratch his back. "What's the matter?" Lauren exclaimed.

"Ooo, it itches, it itches!" the other Underling complained. "My back is itchy!"

And soon enough, it seemed that all the Underlings were itching and scratching and climbing up for some fresh air, but the children could not pay too much attention to them, for the ice beneath the yak's heavy steps suddenly gave a groan and a creak. The yak stopped in his tracks. He began to snort and back up, almost falling over the boat that was behind him.

"It's okay," Michael called as he leapt down from the yak's back. He quickly untied the boat and the rope and motioned for the yak to turn around. "The ice is melting here," Michael said. "Our footsteps are filling with water." The yak continued to walk backward. The other children slid off his back. "You'd better not come any further, dear yak. We have a boat, but you will sink."

"Yes," sighed the yak, and his face looked very sad indeed.

"Are we still on our way to the castle?" Rukmini asked.

"Yes, yes!" said the yak, and began retreating further. The ice was now quite soggy.

"Climb into the boat!" said Lauren, and they all did, pushing it at the same time to where the solid sea seemed to be turning into liquid again. They turned to look back at the yak. He stood there forlornly in the ice and snow, watching the children with his big, sad, dark eyes.

"I wish we could take him with us," Lauren sighed. "He's such a dear. And he seemed to know where to go."

"Let's draw him before we sail out of sight," Rukmini suggested, "so we can remember him."

Michael pushed the Magic Book in their direction. It was too heavy to lift, so they simply opened it. "Oh, look, Lauren. There are only two pages left! We simply can't draw our dear yak!"

"Why, of course!" Lauren shouted, waving vigorously at the yak with tears in her eyes. "Of course we can draw him! Don't you see? Look at his horns. Look! They're shaped like the letter Y! The yes-yak is a Y! Bye, dear yes-yak! Bye-bye and thank you!" Lauren began to draw the yak, and before her eyes, he emerged on the page almost as real as if he were standing there in the book, living and breathing.

"Thank you, sir!" Michael called as the boat slipped gently away from the packed ice and into the cold, open sea. The yak turned, kicked up snow, and galloped away until he was a mere speck of dark in the world of white behind them.

twenty-six

ZIGZAGGING through the water to avoid massive, floating chunks of ice, the children sailed quietly on. No birds sang, and around them, silence grew. It grew and it grew until it was almost unbearable. There was no color in the world, no light, no sound, just a misty nothingness, a cold emptiness, until Rukmini said at last in a tiny voice, "only one page left."

The children looked at one another and then down at the Magic Book, which, because it was so heavy, had to be kept in the center of the boat. Around them, it felt as though it should be night, but they couldn't tell. There was no way of knowing where the sun was. Behind them, they left a thin trail of white foam in the freezing, dark sea; in front of them the water and ice spread out like a blotchy, inky carpet that could easily swallow them and leave not a trace. It was as though all the ink in the world, every single drop, was contained in the dense, deep waters and would gladly seep over anything.

Suddenly, in the distance, something caught Sipho's eye. "Is that a cloud?" he asked.

"I can't see it!" Rukmini said. "Where?"

"High up—right there. It looks like…no, it *is* a turret!"

"It's some kind of spire!"

"It's our eyes playing tricks on us. It can't be real!"

"I see it too! It *is* real!"

"Could it be …?"

"No!" cried Rukmini. "It can't possibly be. We can't be there yet. We only have twenty-five letters. We have to have twenty-six before we arrive. It must be a trick!"

"But look, it's so beautiful!" Lauren gasped. "It looks like it's made of glass and light."

There was a tiny gap in the clouds just above the tallest spire. A single ray of sunlight shone down through the gap and turned the spire into a brilliant rainbow, which vanished almost as soon as it appeared. For a moment, it looked like dying evening light. Then the gap in the clouds closed, as mysteriously as it had opened. Darkness seeped across the world behind them, and the children could see their own shadows growing longer.

There were no waves, but suddenly the boat lurched to the left.

"I think we've hit a rock!" Michael said.

Then the boat lurched to the right. Rukmini ran to the edge and peered over.

"Oh," she choked. The boat lurched again—left, then right. "It's Urckl!" She cried. The monster's name hung in the air, which suddenly became too thick to breathe. The sea was so black now that she could see nothing beneath the surface. The boat lurched again. This time water poured in over the side.

Sensing danger, the Underlings crept out from their comfortable folds and creases and bags. They perched on shoulders, on the sails of the boat, anywhere high.

The dormouse climbed out of the bag and ran up the mast, where he hung on for dear life.

Then, everyone saw what they had been dreading all along. A few hundred feet away, an inky, slimy, scaly tail thrashed up out of the water, sending a shower of cold sea over everyone. There was a thunderous roar and a splash, and then, right next to the little boat, something exploded out of the sea. It was so hideous that no light had ever revealed it. The children gazed at it for a few frozen moments. Then it sank back down again into the water, sending the boat rocking far over the waves.

"Help!" Lauren tried to call out, but her voice stopped in her throat.

"Hold onto the Magic Book!" Michael called as the bottom of the boat was bumped and thumped from underneath. It rocked to the left and right, waves splashing into it from both sides.

"The book's too heavy!" said Sipho. "What are we to do?"

"What about the Magic Opal?" Rukmini asked Lauren, and began to cry.

"Good idea!" Lauren whispered, and fumbled for it. She held it up and tried to see into it.

"Tell us what you see!" Michael said, battling to untangle himself from the sail.

"I see…oh it looks like the dragon-ship! And…and…."

Then, with a splatter and a groan, which sounded like the breaking of a thousand ships, the monster beneath the boat lifted the small vessel high into the air and dropped it. The last thing the children saw as the boat turned upside down and plunged downward, was the Magic Book, all twenty five of its pages fluttering wildly as it fell toward the darkness of the deep.

The children were freezing and coughing and wet and afraid and looking for one another as they came to the surface of the water—so far apart that none could see the other.

The sea rocked and churned and boiled as if this was indeed the end of the world.

Suddenly, through the darkness, the children saw a ghostly white form on the horizon. It was a ship—a ship they recognized, floating rapidly and silently toward them, with a stern dragonhead at its prow and a lady in white at its helm.

The lady in white reached down, and threw out into the sea, one, two, three, four, five ropes. They uncoiled through the air like enormous gossamer spider's webs, and caught each of the children and the dormouse, sticking to them fast, and drawing them swiftly toward the ship.

Once on deck, the children wept and embraced one another and the dormouse, and turned, dripping and cold, to thank the white lady, old Dame Gothel.

"My dears," she said, "you've done such good work."

"Oh, but we haven't," cried Lauren. "It's all lost now. It's all over! And all of the Underlings have vanished!" She buried her face in her hands and wept.

They felt a bump beneath the hull, and another. "Oh no!" they shrieked in one voice. A black shape swirled up through the water at the side of the ship. Suddenly, Sipho thought of the gift he'd received. He unbuttoned his wet pocket and reached inside and took out the beautiful xylophone. There was a flash, like a distant flicker of lightning, and the xylophone stood there in front of him, as large as its original size. *That is the music that could melt the heart of a monster*, he remembered Madame Conch Ends saying. So he began to play. The music rose up from the ship and floated out over the water, hovering there for a while in an echo that everyone could almost see. Sipho played on and on, and as he played, it was as if the thick oily water began to lose its density. The air lost its heaviness.

The others looked over the edge of the ship. For a moment, they saw the enormous dark, hideous shape of the monster. They saw his long tail and gigantic limbs and the head that had reared at them so terrifyingly out of the water. Then the water shimmered. No one could see exactly what was happening, but it looked as if the monster's limbs became rounder, and then drifted away like great globs of oil. Where his giant tail had been, a dark patch of bubbles rose to the surface of the sea and burst. The children watched in awe as the dense darkness became lighter.

"He is, after all, only a creation. If cold, cruel, ignorant hearts and minds can allow such a monster to form, then warm, kind, knowing hearts can uncreate him...," said old Dame Gothel.

They watched as all the darkness under the boat finally dissolved first into black shadows and then into oily patches that evaporated in the sun.

The sun!

It began to break through the clouds and the children felt its warmth on their cheeks, as though someone were gently touching them. Unaccustomed to the light, their eyes could scarcely bear its brilliance. All around them, the sound of dripping and cracking could be heard as great lumps of ice, both near and far, melted and splashed into the sea.

"There it is!" Rukmini gasped. "The castle of the Wise Enchanter!"

Across the water, rising up out of the evaporating fog and drifting mists, stood a castle so beautiful that words could not capture its magnificence. The sun reflected off its high glass spires and turrets. Ahead, the children could see a golden beach. Beyond that, behind the castle, they could see that the hills that had been covered with snow and ice were now beginning to turn green.

"So here we are," Lauren said in a small voice, "without the Magic Book and only twenty five out of twenty six letters...and...no Underlings!" Everyone was solemnly silent.

The dragon-ship sped toward the beach and old Dame Gothel reached for an anchor made of pure, solid gold. "Help me lift this, children. We'll have to walk through the water for the last bit of the journey."

It took all of them and the dormouse to heave the anchor over the side of the ship. As they watched it descend, they marveled at how clear the water was. It was as pure and still as blue-green glass.

By now the mist had completely evaporated. The children and the dormouse climbed down from the ship into the water and waded through the transparent, blue sea toward the beach. There, suddenly, a wide pathway appeared. It zigzagged from the sand, up through an undulating green lawn, to a door in the palace studded with enormous jewels.

"The pathway is a zigzag! Z!" shouted Michael. And his voice caught in his throat as he turned to look at his friends.

"We have the twenty-sixth letter!" Rukmini exclaimed. "We've found the last one! Oh!" she put her hand over her mouth quickly, so she wouldn't say anymore.

"The final letter," Sipho said softly. "And too late for us. Too late."

The four children stood there gazing quietly at the pathway.

"It's never too late," whispered a voice somewhere overhead. Sipho looked up. The others looked up. Old Dame Gothel's mouth dropped open in surprise. "Never too late, never too late…" the whisper echoed through the sky. Laughter shimmered in the air.

"The Underlings!" Lauren exclaimed.

"They have wings!" Michael cried. "They're all green and yellow and shining!"

"They're carrying something!" Rukmini said, hopping from one foot to the other.

"Drop it, folks, drop it!" cried the leader of the Underlings from the air.

There was a thud as the Magic Book fell into the sand and landed open on the very last page.

With a whirring of wings, two hundred and one Underlings landed on the shoulders of the four children. They watched carefully as the picture of the last letter, the zigzag pathway to the castle in front of them, was drawn by *everyone's* hands in the final page of the Magic Book. The drawing seemed to finish itself beneath the children's fingers.

When it was done, the children looked at it in awe for a long time and then shut the Magic Book.

"What happened?" Lauren finally asked the Underlings.

"Well, we weren't always Underlings," one said. "We were air-spirits, thank-you-very-much, until Urckl started getting strong. It got so cold and the air got so heavy that our wings just shriveled up, so we had to go live Underneath."

"We knew the Wise Enchanter could help us, but we didn't know how to find him," said another.

"But our wings had begun to grow back already because of your warmth and kindness," said another on Rukmini's shoulder. "We felt wings itching and itching to grow when we were all riding on the yak."

"Yes!" said the leader. "And when the monster lifted the boat up, and our bodies felt air rushing through them, our wings unfolded in an instant and we caught the Magic Book as it fell to the sea!"

"Oh my dear, dear Underlings, I beg your pardons, air-spirits I should say. You've saved the journey for us. But what about the Wise Enchanter?" Lauren asked carefully.

"He's waiting for you," said a lovely, musical voice. The children turned. Across the beach walked the most beautiful woman that anyone had ever seen. She had long golden brown hair and a diamond crown on her head, and the smile on her face was as warm as the sun. She came to stand before them. "My name is Gadrun. I am the Wise Enchanter's daughter, and also the dolphin you met at the start of your journey, and the one you rescued in the cleft in the rocks. I owe you my thanks. Let me show you to my father."

Michael bent down to pick up the Magic Book. "Either this isn't so heavy anymore, or I'm getting stronger," he said. The others laughed with delight.

"I believe someone needs my help at sea," said old Dame Gothel suddenly. "I'll return shortly, if you don't mind." The children waved and then watched as Gadrun began to walk, or glide rather, along the zigzagging path that lead to the great castle doors.

epilogue

THEY WALKED IN SILENCE—first this way, and then that way—and turned again until they stood in front of the gleaming gemstone doors. Gadrun raised her hand and the doors swung open. The children, with Rukmini carrying the dormouse, entered behind her and found themselves in a vast hall paved entirely with gold.

"Welcome," she said softly.

An enormous bed, made of pink and purple amethyst, stood at the other end of the hall. The children followed Gadrun toward it, all the way across the floors of gold. They hardly dared breathe as they looked on the face of the ancient man who lay there on the bed.

His eyes were closed. His face was as old as Time and reminded Rukmini of her grandfather, and even her grandmother. Looking at his face Michael thought of the Hermit, and Sipho of Madame Conch Ends. Then the ancient man spoke, and his voice was rich with all the pictures, all the words, and all the Wisdom that was ever in the world.

"Thank you for coming." His voice carried like the music of the tide. "You've brought me the book. Let me hold it."

Michael placed the Magic Book on the Wise Enchanter's bed. Slowly, the Wise Enchanter reached over to touch it. As he did so, he took a deep breath and opened his eyes. Then he smiled and, a few seconds later, sat up. "Ah! That feels so much better," he said, looking at the children. As he did so, his eyes sparkled like pieces of bright blue sky.

He began to look through the book slowly from the first page to the last. When he got to the last page, it began to shimmer and glow. The zigzagging path on the paper seemed to be made of real gold. Then, he carefully closed the book. He swung his legs off the bed and rose up tall, so very tall that the children gasped. His cloak was at once cloth and air and mist. He walked and he also floated. His laugh rang through the golden hallway. Finally, he came to each child in turn and shook his or her hand.

Gadrun walked by her father's side and her eyes shone with delight.

"You've been courageous," the Wise Enchanter said solemnly, "And neither selfish, nor unkind. Because of your deeds in the world, my strength is returning. Dear children, in this Magic Book, and now in your hearts, are all the seeds of the Wisdom of the world. The Magic Book will remain here. But you will carry the Wisdom with you out into the world."

"And now," he said, "tell me your questions. I know all your hearts were full of questions before your journey began. What is the question in your heart, Michael?"

"Well, I've wanted to know for some time, why the sky is blue."

"Close your eyes and look into your heart," the Wise Enchanter said, "and you will find the answer."

"I think that the sky is blue because the sun loves it so much that it sends millions of rays through the darkness and turns it to light."

"Ah, good answer," he said and, at that moment, Michael understood something quite suddenly.

"Oh sir! Oh, Rukmini, Sipho, and Lauren. Listen! Madame Conch Ends isn't a real name...we just weren't ready to understand it. I understand it now, her name. It's Conscience."

"Conscience, yes," the Wise Enchanter said, and smiled. "She is now returning to the world and if you listen carefully, you will always hear her whispering in your ear. Don't forget her, children."

"No," they all said together. "We will never forget her, our dear Madame Conscience."

"And now, Rukmini, what is your question?"

"I want to know what the biggest number in the whole world is."

"Look inside," the Wise Enchanter said. Rukmini closed her eyes.

"Maybe," said Rukmini suddenly, "the biggest number in the whole world is...one! Everything and everyone is contained in one big world, you see. Everything can always be in one!"

"Yes! Wonderful. Lauren, what's your question?"

"Why do my eyes blink?"

"Close them and see."

"They blink," she said slowly, "because my body must close its windows sometimes, so that I can know light from darkness."

"Aha," said the Wise Enchanter quietly, "very wise indeed. And you, Sipho?"

"Is there someone who knows everything in the world?"

"Tell me," said the Wise Enchanter. Sipho closed his eyes for a very long time. Finally he opened them.

"I don't know," he said softly. "I think I would have to live from the beginning of time to the end to know the answer to that question."

"Indeed," said the Wise Enchanter. "Yes indeed, my dear Sipho." His eyes shone with kindness and delight, and he seemed to grow even taller. "Any other questions?"

"Um, about the dormouse," Rukmini said. "Can he stay with us?"

"In your world, as it stands, animals don't have the power of speech," the Wise Enchanter said. "Once, long ago, this may have been different, but some things that are lost or stolen are not found again. As you must return, it will be up to him to decide whether he would like to live as ordinary animals do."

"I love to speak," said the dormouse. "Love it." They looked at one another sadly. "I just can't see myself as an ordinary pet," he whispered